Please return/renew this item by the last date shown. Books may also be renewed by phone or internet.

 www.rbwm.gov.uk/home/leisure-and-culture/libraries

☎ 01628 796969 (library hours)

☎ 0303 123 0035

D1380465

Delphi

Delphi

CLARE POLLARD

FIG TREE
an imprint of
PENGUIN BOOKS

FIG TREE

UK | USA | Canada | Ireland | Australia
India | New Zealand | South Africa

Fig Tree is part of the Penguin Random House group of companies
whose addresses can be found at global.penguinrandomhouse.com.

Penguin
Random House
UK

First published 2022
001

Set in 12.5/14.75pt Garamond MT Std
Typeset by Jouve (UK), Milton Keynes
Printed and bound in Great Britain by Clays Ltd, Elcograf S.p.A.

The authorized representative in the EEA is Penguin Random House Ireland,
Morrison Chambers, 32 Nassau Street, Dublin D02 YH68

A CIP catalogue record for this book is available from the British Library

ISBN: 978-0-241-55853-9

www.greenpenguin.co.uk

For Hannah

Note: All characters in this novel are fictitious.

Kassandra: [scream] [scream] [scream] [scream]

                     – Anne Carson

Theomancy:
Prophecy by Foretelling Events

I am sick of the future. Up to here with the future. I don't want anything to do with it; don't want it near me.

No one used to have to deal with this much future. I mean, the future, so far as they could imagine, would have been fairly like the past: harvest, solstice, snow, trees coming into bud. They would get older and die, but the cycle would begin again. We have to live with this rising tide of future, leaking and sopping over everything, claiming cities and sectors, until we're in the future, already – that dystopian future of surveillance, video calls and VR headsets, and viral epidemics spread by globalization, and the 24-hour news saying AI extinction event gene-modification the collapse of civilization.

So it is that, somehow, one winter night, I find myself standing in my kitchen, hissing shrilly at my husband: *I don't know if my son will even live to middle age.*

*

Something can be melodramatic and true at the same time.

In Delphi, gods spoke through oracles. Delphi is in Greece, on multiple plateaux along the slope of Mount Parnassus. The myth says that Zeus wanted to find the centre of Gaia – the Greek personification of the Earth, our primordial mother – so sent two eagles soaring from the east and west. The spot where their flight paths crossed over Delphi was declared the navel of Gaia, sometimes also known as the Omphalos.

Delphi belonged to Gaia, then, but Apollo slayed the dragon who guarded it, the Python (from the verb *pythō*, 'to rot'), and stole the land from her. To legitimize his theft, a sanctuary was built for him above the deep, zigzagged chasm into which he had pushed the Python's dying body. There they later installed the Pythia, a priestess named after that rotting-dragon smell. The famous oracle of Delphi. By custom, she was an older woman – what we might call middle-aged – and often poor. Someone who had led an ordinary life but who was willing to sever ties with her husband or children completely and erase herself. To become a blank; become instrument.

Before the oracle could begin there was a ritual: priests sprinkled a goat with cool water. If it didn't shiver there would be another month's wait; if it shivered, they could proceed, sacrificing it and burning the flesh. Rising smoke signalled the oracle was open.

Next, the Pythia was purified by fasting and bathing in a spring. They seem to have burned laurel leaves to cleanse her, or else she chewed them. Purple veiled, she was taken down into a dark, enclosed inner sanctum and placed on a gilded tripod that teetered over the fissure. I wonder if her heart was panting? I wonder if she was afraid? The room was low and dim, she trembled as fumes rose from the decomposing dragon; sly, sweet, lifting vapours that lurched her into a blood-thumping blur or violent trance, her limbs loosened from her own control.

She jangled above the pit, enlarging. Apollo moved the bones of her jaw, her clump of tongue, to speak through her mouth – a male voice issuing furious barks, a roar.

The historian and essayist Plutarch, who worked as a priest at Delphi, attributed her ecstasies to the *pneuma*: the breath of the fault in the rock. He wrote rather memorably that she looked like a windswept ship.

It was probably anaesthetic, the rock's breath – sugared ethylene or ethane, a heavy, crawling asphyxiant. The sanctuary lacked oxygen. And therefore, lo: the future spilt from her mouth –

Theia Mania:
Prophecy by Divine Madness

The philosopher Thomas Hobbes suggests that our urge to look into the future is rooted in our terror of 'death, or poverty, or another calamity'; that this fear gnaws at us like the eagle gnawed Prometheus' liver.

I'm not sure. Teenagers, for example, swoon over stars in magazines because they *want* the future. When we are young, we visit the palmist to hear of tall, dark men and dazzling success – to imagine ourselves as adults finding love, adventure, vocation. Predictions are a form of day-dreaming, of dragging the future a little closer. They were for me at least. I kept a dream journal with a dream dictionary next to it; bought tarot cards; even tried to cast a few spells, as if the future could be summoned. Supposedly the most basic spell is the 'glamour', but I had a hooked nose and hairy arms and it didn't seem to work that well for me.

One of the few things I know about my father is that he said he was psychic. Is that why I've always sought out oracles? Perhaps it's in my blood. My father died when I was two, I don't remember him. Apparently he was fun, what people call 'the life and soul'. His party trick was reading palms and when he read my mother's he said:

You're going to marry me. He drank himself to death on purpose. He said he didn't want to stop – he knew he was going to die, must have felt it in his insides, but he chose to keep on drinking as though it was his destiny. As though he couldn't cheat the gods. A kind of self-fulfilling prophecy, I suppose, like that of the Italian astrologer Girolamo Cardano, who committed suicide to prove his prediction he would die at the age of seventy-six correct.

*

Clairvoyance can be divided into roughly three classes.

Retrocognition: the ability to see past events.

Remote viewing: the perception of contemporary events outside the range of normal perception.

Precognition: the ability to predict future events.

When Croesus, king of Lydia, sent emissaries to seven oracles, to ask each on the same day what the king was doing at that very moment, the Delphic Pythia famously declared: 'I count the grains of sand on the beach then measure the sea; I understand the dumb so hear the voiceless.'

After this, she correctly reported that the king was making a lamb-and-tortoise stew. I would class this as remote viewing.

Oracles were most keenly sought, though, for their precognition, despite the fact that the prophecies of oracles could be mainly understood as the gods explaining their intentions verbatim. Famous proclamations such as 'Love of money will ruin Sparta' or 'If you cross the river a great empire will be destroyed' can, in other words, be understood as the gods saying: 'Do what we wish or we will punish you.'

Oracles didn't, then, quite predict the future. They only provided intelligence about the plans of the most powerful, though these were, admittedly, so likely to come true as to be easily mistaken for prophecy. It was like hearing men behind closed doors, before an election, saying they are going to hack and leak, target misinformation at black women, blackmail X, disenfranchise Y, and knowing their desire will come to pass. *A great democracy will be destroyed.*

To overhear such things, it seems, made mortals mad. Divine madness, or what Plato describes as *Theia Mania*. Some report that what the Pythia uttered were in fact incomprehensible sounds that the priests would 'translate' into hexameters. We must not forget these machinations of the propaganda machine. As a translator myself, I find it highly likely that meaning might have changed to fit the form, not to mention suit the purposes of those translating. Language is always power. As Plato also said, 'Those who tell the stories rule society.'

Haruspicy: Prophecy by Entrails

I am researching prophecy in the Ancient World, for what I hope might be my next book. A Classical Reception Studies sort of thing, chapters about changing depictions of Cassandra and astrology and so on. Wikipedia says: 'Because of the high demand for oracle consultations and the oracles' limited work schedule, they were not the main source of divination for the Ancient Greeks. That role fell to the seers.' Wikipedia is obviously not an appropriate source for academic work, but the tone makes me smile: 'the oracles' limited work schedule'.

Seers didn't contact the gods, then. Nothing bright or monstrous sluiced through them. They just interpreted signs, like jobbing tradesmen diagnosing a problem with your electrics. Though more numerous and accessible, they were a basic service, only able to answer yes-or-no questions; often having to kill several creatures to get a consistent answer.

Haruspicy: divination by entrails.

In *Electra*, Euripides claims that Prometheus handed this art to man, a sacrilegious act for which Zeus punished him. The seers would perform the *hiera* by slaughtering a sheep at the camp ground, then digging around in the smoked mirror of its liver for the answer: inspecting the size of the lobe, looking for a river or path, the cleft or gate in smooth, quivering meat. Following this was the ritual of the *sphagia*, often near the intended battlefield – slitting the throat of a young female goat before taking notes on its final stumbling steps, the patterned splattered blood and shit.

The seer would scratch his head and say: *A tricky one, this.* The question was always how to win.

Rhapsodomancy: Prophecy by Poetry

The guy I called 'dad' when I was small was this snivelling creep called Steve. I spent my adolescence hating the present: PE, the cat-food smell of my kitchen, my mother divorcing Steve, my mother watching *Jerry* fucking *Springer* and bingeing on biscuits, the friends I had nothing in common with, Australian soaps, the mediocre minds of boys.

But my sixth form taught Latin, even though it was a state school. I'd always loved myths and legends; had gulped down all Robert Graves' Claudius books. I was top of my year at German, with a talent for languages. We had this wonderful Latin teacher, Mrs Sykes – a skinny, husky smoker who only wore black – who read out Ovid and Catullus with relish; told us how Romans would wash their clothes in urine and eat flamingo.

The luck, in a certain light, looked as though the three Fates were spinning my thread. I remember asking the tarot cards if I would get in to Oxford to study Classics and it was a yes.

Having won a place at New College, I felt self-conscious at first, being so conspicuously not posh (from Barnsley of all places). Still, I was in my future, and it was so different to my previous life I couldn't help but enjoy it. My bad skin retreated and I got that rose-scented cream for your lip that burns the hair off. I suddenly felt attractive – in this change of context I wasn't even the swot but a bit of rough! Sipping college port with self-satisfied old men, deliberately shocking them with my working-class honesty. Sleeping with boys and girls in wood-panelled rooms, the scout tiptoeing in to empty our bins. O careless Mark, whose parents had a boathouse; that German student who lifted weights and came in my mouth; Pandora, with her expensively groomed hair, the sort she'd casually put up without even looking in a mirror . . .

I loved the library; its stacks; the classical reading rooms. The willows. Pimm's with chopped bits of fruit. I loved Greek tragedies best. The term 'tragedy', τραγῳδία, means 'song of the goats'. I loved the chorus; the catharsis. The boy's body lying prey for carrion; the long golden pins from Jocasta's dress. Medea lifted by the 'mechane' device in Helios' chariot. Cassandra crying: *Aieeeeeeee!*

In the final term I started dating Jason, who was handsome in an almost clichéd sort of way with big features: a big chin, big man's hands. Golden hair, and because he was tall in my mind he was always stooping over me with the light pouring through it. He was toned from sport then; dabbling with running and rowing. A soft, easy gaze and self-deprecatingly witty; always knew where the parties were. He had started to DJ – House or UK Garage, dance stuff – and I remember him always shouting inside my ear, the intense tickle of it; bone-juddering kisses that tasted of vodka and energy drinks. We fucked in long grass near the riverbank one night under the wheel of stars, and I felt like Demeter lying with Iasion. 'I love you,' he said, and then my name. It gave me a feeling of predestination.

That last summer I wore my hair short and a lilac ball gown, and walked home barefoot after the sun had risen, my feet bleeding from high heels. So much champagne. Everybody touching casually in the rinsing sunlight.

Genethlialogy:
Prophecy by Birth Dates

But the past is always more beautiful than the present.

Entropy is the progression from order to disorder.

Since the Big Bang things have become progressively more disordered.

The second law of thermodynamics states that entropy can only increase within a system. This is why time can only move forward.

Things can only get more complicated and fucked up.

I sip cold coffee, click on *Consciousness could be a side effect of 'entropy' say researchers: what if disorder maximizes the brain's information content?* Perhaps the deeper into the future we get, the more aware of it we become.

Perhaps this is our curse.

Recently, I have begun to fear the future. This year I am forty-five, and for the last decade I have taught Classics on a part-time contract at a good university; have translated, from the German, some prize-winning novels, although my name is rarely mentioned in the reviews. I am, I suppose, at the peak of my career. But both my jobs feel underpaid and undervalued, reliant on me putting in wageless hours through love. It didn't used to bother me when I was young and grateful, but I'm becoming more conscious.

Tarotmancy: Prophecy by Tarot

I try to count my blessings.

My son, Xander, is one of them, though he rarely does anything but 'game' now he's ten. His longish dark curls tucked behind his ears (he hates the hairdresser's); his fingers in their furious, jerky dance. Xander has always been sore with eczema and allergies, uncomfortable in his body – I remember him in his Moses basket, screaming like he was being boiled, his scratch mitts clawing the air. Only the virtual world seems to offer escape. But his teachers say he's polite; good at maths and art. I love his deadpan humour and his soft brown stare.

Jason works long hours for a charity these days, and he doesn't look after his health – running to fat; his face is getting redder somehow, and coarser; his hair thin – but he's good company, full of bonhomie, always inviting people over for dinner, putting vinyl on the turntable, planning some nice treat or trip. We holiday a couple of times a year in Italy or Ibiza, with wine on a whitewashed terrace; snorkelling in sunlit pale-green water. Him pulling apart a big, sticky prawn with his fingers or tucking into a fritto misto, saying *this is the life*.

I'm middle class now, I suppose, although I always say that reluctantly – angry at how the media equate the middle class with private schools, second homes, nannies, cleaners, all this privileged shit neither I nor anyone in my family has ever been able to afford, rather than highly skilled precarious work that barely hits the median wage. But unlike my younger colleagues we're homeowners with a spare room; we order takeaways; we buy eight-pound bottles of wine. I feel the weight of my luck at night.

It is not going to get better than this. I will age and diminish. And the world, too, diminishes. I'm not sure how long my department will exist. What jobs will even exist by the time Xander is an adult. How many holidays abroad we might have left. How many fish are left in that pale-green water. I am unsure what to aim for. To look forward to.

The last time I shuffled my deck and laid out a tarot spread was when we were trying for Xander. I laid the last card, what will be, and it was the Ten of Cups.

X marks the spot.

Beneath the rainbow, a man and a woman; his arm around her. They are in a beautiful garden; two children, a girl and a boy, skip with joy.

Contentment, repose of the entire heart; the perfection of that state.

I hoped this meant two children but it didn't. She was a miscarriage, my daughter. But that reading was always too literal. I still have a good life. Perhaps it's better, not having a second child who might have had the same suffering skin and short breath. Every stupid little nut making my heart freefall in my chest. *In childbirth grief begins.*

Still, still, this is the golden time: privilege, garden, home, family. I should be happy with what I have. But I keep thinking of the end of *Oedipus Rex*: 'Mortals must always look towards their end. None can be called happy until the day they carry that happiness into a peaceful grave.'

Why am I dissatisfied, wanting to throw away this happiness when I should be trying to carry it carefully to the grave with me? Why do I want to have an affair, leave, quit my job, anything?

Because otherwise nothing will ever happen again.

Ovomancy: Prophecy by Eggs

From the first moment I hear about the virus I know it is coming for us, I can feel it creeping closer. I start checking my phone almost every half-hour. 'You're getting carried away, come on,' Jason says, as I read about the Huanan seafood wholesale market. In Wuhan people are being turned away from hospitals; are boarded into flats to die.

'We won't be able to go to Greece at Easter,' I tell him. I've booked flights. I want to visit Delphi, where I've never been, then stay for a week at Galaxidi; drink coffee and ouzo on terraces by the sea.

'Don't be so dramatic.'

'I'm not being.'

'What, they're going to just "stop" travel? How's that going to work? I mean, if they can't contain the virus then that's it. Once it's everywhere, it's everywhere, right?'

'I think the holiday has to actually be cancelled for us to get our money back, the government need to ban flights.'

'Oh, right, well that's not happening, is it, so just chill, will you?'

A week later the virus is in Italy, in ski lodges, on planes. My premonition soon proves correct. It's disappointing, but in a way I am also thrilled because something is happening. Everyone is thrilled, actually! We are so bored of our unreal lives it is a change, at least; it is history happening.

People start to panic buy. The Germans have a word for it, this hoarding: *Hamsterkauf.* Like a little hamster stuffing up its cheeks with food for later. Secretly, I quite enjoy stocking up, high on the artifice of the gesture. At first I just put the odd extra in the supermarket shop: a block of halloumi, a can of beans, frozen spinach. Then it mounts. Five packets of macaroni, a mixed box of British fish, a huge tile of eggs, repurposed from catering supplies (the only eggs left in the store). I am a good little hamster. Jason buys three chorizos and a bottle of vodka.

Then suddenly it's too close. At the play park a mum whose child is sucking the bar on the roundabout says her friend is a doctor and thinks everyone will have it by the end of the month. Another friend texts that he is struggling to breathe, with severe stomach pain; the ambulance comes but they won't take him, just tell him to lie on the kitchen tiles with his body flat. A young black woman dies down the road after being told she isn't a priority. Apparently if you phone the hospital they say if you can speak words you can't come in. I remember them saying that when I was giving birth; it sounds like some terrifying reversed labour. Someone is permitted to phone when your lips turn blue.

At night the sirens howl: *Aieeeeeeee!*

Ophthalmomancy: Prophecy by Eyes

'I'm worried about Xander,' I tell Jason in the kitchen, stirring as he pours out the wine. 'His asthma.'

'They say it doesn't affect children, right?'

'They don't know really, though, do they? He has an underlying condition. You know: underlying condition – what they say after they announce the number of deaths, like a little excuse note.'

'What d'you want to do?' Jason asks. 'I'm not really up for taking him out of school, to be honest, I mean, who'd look after him? It could be weeks. I've got a deadline at the end of the month.'

'I know, I just . . .'

The next day they announce the schools are closing and it's decided for me. It occurs to me in some ways that's better. I can keep him safe. No torturous choosing. No nightmares about classmates with peanut-butter fingers from breakfast either. I can make our house into a cocoon for a month or so until it's over. Also, he won't get nits. On the news I hear the word *shielding*.

However, in other ways I soon find I worry more, about looking competent in front of work colleagues; about his development. The deaths start to skitter wildly upwards; the lockdown to unspool ahead of us, getting longer and longer. After a couple of weeks he refuses to read books, suddenly, as if knowing that is a way to wound me, his bookish mother. Sanitizer makes Xander's hands raw; soap makes his hands raw. On daytime TV they explain how you should keep your online groceries in a separate room for seventy-two hours and then wash each piece of fruit individually, and he snaps at me, slightly hysterical: *Mum, you're not washing our shop well enough, you idiot!* Just a couple of years ago he would snuggle up to me in his onesie. *My lovely mum.* Now he doesn't sleep much, his eyes liverish with dark circles.

It doesn't help that his fucking useless school barely does anything, just sends worksheets with things like word searches on them, but our printer is broken so before I start my own work I have to write out all these fucking word searches by hand. There's a Christian word search he laughs at, for RE. He says, 'I think I believe in gods more than God, Mum.'

There are so many meals to make. I seem to always be scraping pasta off the bottom of a pan. Whilst I cook, Xander plays Roblox on the old iPad, its fingerprinted screen dull like the waters of Lethe, or else Fortnite with his headphones on, talking to friends at least, though I keep hearing swear words. Or he watches YouTube videos by these idiot men-children. As he watches other people play games I wonder if he could put himself at any further distance from reality.

'Why don't you practise the drums?' I ask. As if it would be realer, somehow.

'Are you kidding me?' Jason shouts down from the study where he gets the luxury of working all day and also listening in on me. 'I'm about to start a Zoom call, we have neighbours! You're honestly telling him to use his drums now?'

Screenlight. Blue screenlight. That squidgy distractor toy Xander has squeezed for years because of his eczema is never out of his hand, pulsing like an extra organ; like he's weighing up my heart.

Stichomancy: Prophecy by Lines Chosen at Random

And me too, on the screen, of course. Me too, my eyes brimming with blue light. I have a theory about the internet actually – that it's filled a void left by the decline in religion. For centuries humanity always felt it was being watched, and this knowledge gave even our smallest actions a sense of importance. Then, for a while, no one was bearing witness. No one was looking and it made us feel trivial and tenuous; utterly disposable to the indifferent world. That's why we wanted to be on reality TV, so someone would see us. And now social media has filled the void. No evil tweet, it promises, will go unread and unpunished; goodness will be rewarded with 'likes' and supportive Mandela quotes, or photos of cats. Our whole lives will be archived and remembered – it is always looking, watching, tracking. Saving us.

When the pandemic comes, a lot of people become interested in Nostradamus. A meme spreads across social media about a queen (Corona) rising from the east (China) in a twin year (2020) that Facebook has to obscure with a 'false information' tag. It's funny how much traction Nostradamus still has. In his lifetime Nostradamus' predictions often went wrong. Meeting his patron, Queen Catherine de' Medici, in France in 1564 he promised her peace, but there was civil war two years later. He claimed her son Charles would live to ninety, but he died at twenty-four. Still, he churned out so many vague, prophetic quatrains – at least 6,338 prophecies in total – that some shit was going to stick to the wall eventually.

It seems he used a mash-up of techniques, mixing some astrology with the paraphrasing of many prophetic books and creative licence. The latest research suggests that he may in fact have used stichomancy – randomly selecting a book of history or prophecy and taking his cue from the lines or verses he saw when it fell open. One of the cleverest things he did was to leave his prophecies undated. Most basically, a prediction without a date can never be disproved as time is infinite.

Some claim Nostradamus correctly predicted airlines ('People will travel safely through the sky'), the Great Fire of London ('The blood of the just will be demanded of London burnt by fire in three times twenty plus six'), Spanish flu ('The dreadful war which prepared in the West, the following year the pestilence will come, so very horrible that neither young, nor old, nor animal survive') and the rise of Hitler (Nostradamus calls him 'Hister'). Maybe 9/11 if you squint ('The sky will burn at forty-five degrees, fire approaches the great New City. Immediately a huge scattered flame leaps up').

He knew about plagues, anyway. He was very experienced with plagues. Nostradamus first became famous as an apothecary, creating a 'rose pill' that protected against the plague. Then his first wife and two children died during a plague outbreak in 1534. And is this Nostradamus' premonition of Covid-19? 'In the feeble lists, great calamity through America and Lombardy. Fire in the ship, plague and captivity.' America and Italy; plague and captivity. Are the ships those cruise liners, stranded at sea as death tore through them?

Those cruise liners. I predict someone is going to make a very good movie about Covid-19 sweeping through a cruise liner.

Fructomancy: Prophecy by Fruit

The trouble with how much information there is now is that it's become very hard to like yourself. In ancient times if you were a respectful daughter, a benevolent mother, did your civic duty and made a gift before the shrine of your choice, you could probably consider yourself good. In a globalized world, though, there are few purchases or gestures that do not – like the flicker of a butterfly's wings – negatively affect someone on earth. Switching on a light, buying a friend a coffee, pulling on a T-shirt, driving to school pick-up, buying raspberries out of season, watching a panel show with no black people – with almost every daily action I contribute to world misery. If to be good is not to harm others, then I live within a system that has made goodness impossible.

There's a German word: *Weltschmerz*. 'World pain'. *Du hast Weltschmerz*. And I know it is my fault. Mainly, I just try not to think about it. When I buy apples in a plastic bag because they're cheaper, I just deliberately empty my head. It's kind of like my meditative practice.

Once the pandemic starts, though, I almost feel something new is happening. I am taking in so much information I almost feel good about it. Clean, like there is a moral imperative to be permanently scrolling the *Guardian*'s coronavirus live feed: keeping track of Hong Kong, Brazil, the mass graves in Iran, *Overwhelmed Indian Hospitals Turn Patients Away*. All events are predetermined, in the sense that they are caused by those that precede them. In the early nineteenth century Pierre-Simon Laplace imagined that a 'demon' with perfect understanding of all existing things, as well as the links between them, would therefore be able to form perfect knowledge of the future.

In some foolish way it is as if I am trying to become that demon. If I scroll enough news the future will appear clearly before me.

The internet is suddenly full of conspiracy theories too, perhaps the result of other people trying to join the dots. 5G masts are attacked. Bill Gates wants to plant us with microchips via covid vaccines. I start hearing about Pizzagate, the conspiracy theory which claims that references to ordering pizza from a popular Washington DC pizza restaurant in the stolen emails of Clinton campaign manager John Podesta are actually a code for a child-trafficking ring. QAnon. They believe that members of an elite cabal extract the chemical adrenochrome from the blood of child victims to extend their lives, and give them a high that is 'intense' and 'exotic'. Someone claims that a video was found on the hard drive of a laptop belonging to Hillary Clinton aide Huma Abedin's husband, former Democratic congressman Anthony Weiner. It shows

Abedin and Hillary Clinton filleting a prepubescent girl's face and using it as a mask before drinking her blood.

It's called Frazzledrip. Frazzledrip! Absurd parody of a Dionysian rite. Masked Maenads in an ecstasy of horror. Dionysus the mad one, the eater of raw flesh. The mask images that circulate are clearly fake but they still give people a high that is 'intense' and 'exotic' and they want more. Their slogan is 'Save the Children'.

It *is* weird, though, isn't it, the way the virus doesn't affect children?

I mean, the disease hasn't been designed, that's baseless conspiracy nonsense, but if it *had* been designed, it would have been like this, to kill off the old and weak and not the children. Could you even imagine the hysteria if it actually affected children? The world is going mad over fictional abducted children. What if we actually thought all our real children would die? Can you picture the chaos? We would believe absolutely anything.

Entomomancy: Prophecy by Insect

Moths lend themselves to metaphor.

Clothes shops are all shut so I get last year's clothes out of the cupboards but they are pocked with tiny, ragged holes. The same but worse. This year's slogan.

In Ancient Mesopotamia, counter-intuitively, if moths were seen in a person's house the owner of that house would become important.

I should like moths, I tell myself. I have always been interested in fragments. Scraps. The holes eaten in texts; the glowing meaningfulness of what is left. Is anything more lovely than Anne Carson's translations of Sappho?

    of gold arms [
    ]
    ]
    doom
    ]

Catoptromancy: Prophecy by Mirrors

That end-of-the-world feeling. There's a Delphic prophecy I keep remembering: 'Your statues stand and pour sweat. They shiver with dread. Black blood drips from the high rooftops. Now they see the necessity of evil. Get out, get out of this sanctum! Drown your soul in grief!'

Mournful streets. The play park is taped off: a chain around the small turret of the climbing frame; the swing seats removed. A queue of people snakes around the whole car park at Sainsbury's. Every day we hear the roll call of dead doctors, nurses, bus drivers, shelf-stackers.

But at the same time that totally normal feeling. Xander in his bedroom says: 'Alexa, play "Happy".'

Jason runs his finger across the dust on our mirror and asks, 'How are we at home more but do less cleaning?'

We binge on TV. You know the sort of thing. Repeats of comforting comedies, *The Crown*, *Tiger King*. In many ways a writer will never be able to truly capture lockdown because they will never be able to capture with the right amount of granular detail the sheer number of television shows that people watch. Six hours and twenty-five minutes each day. Forty-five hours a week. Maybe you could write a paragraph about how many shows people watch but it won't get anywhere near the full scope of it, what it means to live more than six hours a day in fake worlds in which you can't touch or smell or intervene, only watch scripted fates happen to people who can't heed your warnings, before turning over in the evening to watch MPs bullshit their way through a daily briefing in which they try to pretend we don't have the worst death toll in Europe, before turning back to Netflix.

And more than that, the writer won't capture what it means to watch TV for more than six hours a day but also be looking at your phone at the same time, the emails or WhatsApp or online shopping slot; doomscrolling; moving seamlessly from the daily deaths to *Killing Eve* to Amazon Prime without ever having to lean on your partner for a moment's entertainment. 'Shush, will you,' Jason says when I talk over a show. 'I'm trying to listen.'

Everything that wasn't TV is TV now too. Exercise is on-screen. The shops are on-screen. My mum is on-screen. I start to learn Italian on Duolingo. I watch plays on my laptop. People tweet pictures of themselves as famous pieces of art: Titian, Goya, Botticelli's *Birth of Venus*. People tweet pictures of their banana bread; infinite dull beige slices. I scroll through rainbows until my fingers feel cranky.

I think of the priestesses who gave oracles to the sick at Patrae by lowering a mirror into Demeter's well on a rope.

Profits are up in Silicon Valley. I mean, the disease hasn't been designed, that's baseless conspiracy nonsense, but if it *had* been designed, it would have been like this, to force our every interaction online so they can scrape it for data and sell predictions of what we'll do before we know ourselves to shadowy forces. The ones that always ask: *How do I win?*

Anthomancy: Prophecy by Flowers

The university has a lot of Zoom crisis meetings where it's hard to really tell what anyone thinks about anything. The students have all been sent home, and we are trying to go online as fast as we can. I am aware that every word of mine I film now belongs to the university. I spend a lot of time trying to move laundry out of my backdrop. There is a seminar that gets Zoom-bombed, someone shouts the N-word and draws what I can only suppose is meant to be a penis on the screen.

Xander has to make a fact file about Mary Seacole; a mind map based on an abridged version of *Oliver Twist*. To draw and label a diagram of a flower: pistil, sepal, stamen. No one is even going to look at these things – his school says they can't mark work because of the germs on it. He refuses to do maths; he kind of whimpers when I try to make him do it, regressing I think.

I wish he hadn't grown out of playing with toys. Although, having said that, not so long ago Xander was into cars, my lounge snared up like some apocalyptic traffic jam of sentient, self-driving vehicles after all the humans are gone. Given he's asthmatic and cars pump warm particles of burnt oil in his face every day, I spent a lot of time thinking what the fuck am I allowing?

Sharing myths with him felt better. Quite often he'd draw his favourite, Hercules, with these very detailed six-packs and scratches all over from battling the Hydra. So many monsters. I had a lovely Usborne book of children's versions and I'd read Xander myths most nights, cosied up: Bellerophon on the back of Pegasus, aiming his bow at the Chimera. Sometimes we'd act them out with Lego. Or he'd say tell me a story, and I'd tell him about Sibyls or Furies or heroes. The tale of Achilles, prophesized to perish young, whose desperate mother held him by the heel and dipped him into the Styx to try to protect him.

I miss playing. It makes me sad we've grown out of that kind of playing. Now the closest he gets is this computer game called *Monster Quest*, where expansive myths have atrophied to a crude code: buy weapon, kill exquisite creature.

Adults don't play, except that game called Instagram. I don't use it much, or rather, I lurk rather than post because the camera on my phone is shit, but I look at it more during lockdown. Our friends take pictures of the spring – apple blossom and peonies – button-holing me as if to say, *look, real things*, but, of course, as soon as they take a photo and add the Valencia filter they've just made another unreal thing, more pretty bits of information on their location and mood for the cloud. I'm looking at it when Jason says, 'I'm buying Xander a phone,' which means I'm in a position of weakness from the start. I'm annoyed he's said it in front of Xander too, who's doing his spelling and looks up, distracted.

'Cool. Thanks, Dad.' He's trying to sound unbothered, but I can sense his heart jumping up like a dog.

'Oh?' I say. 'Why?'

'Because he needs one, don't you, Xander?'

'I was hoping to hold out until secondary school, to be honest,' I tell Jason, aware the debate is already redundant and I'm just admonishing him.

'Yeah, thanks would be nice. You're always saying you're worried about him missing his friends, they all have them – Jaden, Tyler. I spoke to Tyler's dad in the park about different models. Xander needs to be on the WhatsApp, stay in the loop. See the memes.'

'The memes? What, like the crude little gifs your football lads share on WhatsApp?'

'Tyler and Jaden both have them,' Xander chips in. 'For walking home.'

'For *walking home*?' I say, incredulously. As if expensive devices make ten-year-olds safer. As if anyone's walking anywhere ever again.

I'm suspicious of Tyler, who always has a girlfriend or two, whatever that means when you're ten. Xander says that Tyler has his girlfriend's Instagram password, so he can check her DMs, which is what boyfriends do these days. The girlfriend's account is not even private and I've swiped through her selfies. A face pale as blossom. There is definitely make-up on her eyebrows, a cropped 'top'; they are almost professional-looking except they all feature a radiator.

Ololygmancy: Prophecy by the Howling of Dogs

Tragedy is all about Unity of Place. This year every family gets its own tiny tragedy. A small cast of actors, and social media as the chorus.

Lots of people are finding out they don't really like their flats or marriages or lives all that much. Well, except one annoying friend whose sourdough looks professional, though you mustn't say so or he'll take you blow-by-blow through his eleven-step process. We have a Zoom drink with one couple, Toby and Meesha, on a Thursday after the clap for the NHS, and they have an awful row in front of us. Toby says he is going for a drive to clear his head, though he's drunk too much and non-essential journeys are banned, and she slaps him and we think he's going to choke her. At one point we are screaming at them to stop screaming. It's like that film *The Devil's Advocate*. There's this intensely awful scene where Keanu Reeves' character sees his wife commit suicide by cutting her throat with a shard of glass, but she's behind a glass panel and he can't stop her. Zoom starts to feel a lot like that.

Domestic violence is on the rise. Did you know Hercules actually killed his family? His wife and children. Euripides wrote a tragedy about it. Hera poisoned Hercules' wine, and he thought he saw them turn into wild animals that were going to eat him, so lashed out. He was so strong, he killed them all. *Where did this madness grasp me? How? Where was I when it came and destroyed me?*

Home. The sameness of it. The word no longer cosy, a place to return to, but a word that has you caught like a maw. Drawing the curtains and opening the curtains. Changing the sheets. The dust on the grey sofas. The crumbs on the tiles. The damp Victorian walls. The framed *Jason and the Argonauts* poster on the wall. The coarse-grained carpet on the stairs. The sticky ring on the coffee table. *We've made our bed, now lie in it.*

Thousands of tragic deaths, though, occurring beyond the *skênê* of our curtains; our filters. Enter the messenger on Twitter. Or turn on the 24-hour news, that *ekkyklêma* constantly wheeling around to reveal the corpses.

The Prime Minister's been taken to the ICU. He could actually die. Really die, we say to each other. Actually literally die. The atmosphere is charged, some weird mixture of giddy and chastened and afraid of ourselves.

You have to be very careful what you say on Twitter. But people aren't. They say it's faked. They say: 'A man responsible for the deaths of so many and we've to "show respect" cos he's not well, I'll pass.' They say: 'If you can't understand why people are gonna find this funny, I don't know what to tell you.' They say: *Defending the Prime Minister against these sick trolls, Piers Morgan, host of* Good Morning Britain, *demands those who have nothing positive to say should shut up.*

The Furies love Twitter. I think perhaps they are on Twitter. The Erinyes. The Furies with snakes in their hair and their black robes swarming, drinking beyond the limit. When Cronus castrated his father and threw his dick in the sea, they sprang from the drops of blood: Alecto, Megaera, Tisiphone. The dog-faced, blue-ticked dancing troupe; the ones who bay for vengeance.

Augury: Prophecy by Bird Formations

Birdwatching is taking the nation by storm but in my garden there is only ever this one sodding magpie. One day I take Xander up Telegraph Hill and there is a man in joggers holding a kestrel on his fist.

In the evenings I clear out the cupboards. We have these huge cupboards in the eaves of our bedroom, which is a converted loft. Xander used to like playing hide-and-seek in them, snug in the crawl space, but now there are just boxes of his old toys hiding in there; things like a pram and a Moses basket I never threw away, thinking we might have a second child. Moths flutter out, like it's haunted; have eaten the face off a teddy.

Badly paid delivery men chuck cardboard boxes on to doorsteps and back away quickly.

Hermes is always at my door. Hermes, protector of merchants, god of boundaries. Psychopomp delivering our souls into the afterlife and joggers to Xander, who grows out of a pair every week. Hermes, that shapeshifter, who stoops to take a photo.

It is weird, to always be ironing or eating cereal or watching a show actually literally called *Normal People* as the world changes forever.

I'm not paying much attention to Jason. He is an adult, he can sort out himself. Jason is also, of course, male, white, straight, middle class, able-bodied and cis, and as a society we've recently been given a pass on thinking about the inner lives of such people. It has been a while since I've exerted myself to imagine his inner life. We don't have much sex, so he probably masturbates over porn at night, I assume, but I don't think about it.

One time when I masturbate I imagine Zeus in the shape of a swan knocking me to the ground, sunlight pouring through his wings. He penetrates me with his thin corkscrew swan dick.

Turifumy:
Prophecy by Shapes in Smoke

The kids at our uni are told they have to take their finals remotely. There will be no end-of-term parties, no milk round, no celebrations. We have a seminar and half of them have turned their cameras off and I am just staring into all these black screens. I say their names into the darkness. *Jess, what did you find interesting in the text? Are you there, Jess?*

All the department's sums are based on foreign students, and they are worried there won't be any next year. We try to hang on to the ones we've got already at least. I keep having to comfort weeping students over Zoom one-to-ones, checking my own tiny face in the corner for reassurance I am being reassuring enough. But it's fine, I've quickly recalibrated my sense of what is a chore and what is pleasure, so a trip to the park with Xander feels onerous and paid adult labour a treat.

There is a colleague I like. Jay, who used to be a PhD student of mine. Then they were a woman, but now they are non-binary. They interest me. I've never felt I fitted in with other women; have always felt I have a brain that in some ways might read as male. Androgyny, from Ancient Greek ἀνδρόγυνος – *andro* meaning 'man' and *gyné* meaning 'woman'. In Plato's *Symposium*, Aristophanes says male–female people come from the moon.

Jay has a face like the moon, perfectly round, aglow. They always wear crisp shirts with rolled-up sleeves and loose trousers that hang in a stylish way. They have a bob of fine, shiny hair and a cute sort of face with groomed eyebrows and a pierced tongue. Playful, like they want to stick it out at someone. They vape a lot. Flavours like melon and slushie and peanut butter.

It's good to have young people around who look at things differently – Jay's the reason our department issues trigger warnings now. A couple of the older guys complained, but like Jay said, no one's banning Ovid. We're just saying: this might be a bit rapey. It's not like that's a spoiler.

Last year they did a great paper on Tiresias, an oracle who prophesied through the sound of birdsong, the shape of smoke, communication with the dead. The story tells that he beat up these copulating snakes, and an angry Hera punished him by turning him into a woman. Later, Tiresias was drawn into an argument between Hera and Zeus about who had the most pleasure during sex – Hera claimed that the man did, whilst Zeus argued that it was the woman. Tiresias, having experienced sex both ways, was called on for an answer, so replied that: 'Of ten parts, a man enjoys only one.' Women, in other words, get ninety per cent of the pleasure. Outraged, Hera struck him blind for his impiety. It was in recompense for this that Zeus gave Tiresias the gift of foresight.

It's a strange story, isn't it? Did they really believe, the Ancient Greeks, that it was better to be fucked than to fuck? And what a toxic couple anyway, dragging mortals into their slanging match about which one of them enjoyed sex the least.

In our Zoom staff meeting, Jay's upset about the students. They cry. 'These are some of the most important days of their lives,' they say. 'They're struggling with their mental health. Some don't even have decent Wi-Fi. They're trying to do finals in shared bedrooms. They're losing all these special memories, all this joy . . . I mean, they're supposed to give up all the best days of their lives to help the elderly, but no one's even saying thank you. I think a bit more compassion is needed, I mean – we all know there's not even necessarily any jobs at the end of this . . .'

'Okay, we get it, Jay,' the Head of Department nods, leaning back in his chair with a spaced-out grin. 'I think we can safely say we're all scared for our futures, so. It's not just the students who deserve our compassion here, necessarily.' His house is open-plan, and you can hear his wife trying to silence a tantrum about snacks.

Videomancy: Prophecy by Electronic Visual Medium

It's possible to hold two things in your mind at once. To believe in psychics, for example, and at the same time be deeply cynical of psychics. I mean, I'm sure if a colleague asks about my research I will sneer at the idea I believe in such nonsense. I know how language works; how it deceives and manipulates. I know about cold reading. One of the techniques is 'shotgunning', where the psychic offers a huge quantity of general information, observes the subject's reactions, then narrows the scope, refining the original statements according to those reactions.

You live in a house somewhere, right? And I'm getting this really clear sense of someone in the house with you, a husband or – or maybe a cat. Or it could be a pigeon that's accidentally flown in through the window.

And you've suffered a loss, recently, right? A loss very close to you, a relative or – or maybe your car keys? Uh-huh . . . Okay. Some hair came out when you brushed, then, possibly? Or you chucked some old, you know, pesto, one of those bags of salad?

And then there are 'Barnum statements', named after P. T. Barnum, the American showman. They seem personal but apply to almost everyone: 'You're shyer than people think you are'; 'You had an accident when you were a kid, didn't you?' Or the 'rainbow ruse', a statement that covers all possibilities: 'You are a very kind and considerate person, but when somebody does something to break your trust, you feel deep anger.'

I know all this, but at the same time I feel my life has been full of uncanny coincidences. Often, I think of a song and it comes on the radio. Dream of something obscure like marmalade or Tasmania, only to come across an article about it the next day. I still feel a thrill at the black cat crossing my path. I possess a lucky necklace – with a small Greek owl, to symbolize Athena – and when I wear it to exams and interviews they always turn out well. So when someone tweets about a psychic hotline they used I feel a little frisson of fate. I guess it's the boredom of another week of stasis and screens. Also, like every girl brought up to be a good capitalist, I want to be the protagonist of my own life. I want to make a little plot for myself.

*

The Tarot, with its four numbered suits, its face cards, its major arcana, originated in mid-fifteenth-century Europe as a pack of playing cards used for games. The Fool was a kind of top trump or played to avoid following suit. The term Tarot and the German *Tarock* come from the Italian *Tarocchi*. Its origin is uncertain, but *taroch* was a synonym for 'foolishness' – it is a fool's game. It wasn't until the late eighteenth century that the packs began to be used for prediction.

The battered tarot deck I own is the world's most popular seventy-eight-card deck, the Rider–Waite, co-created by A. E. Waite and the artist Pamela Colman Smith in 1909. A few clicks tell me that A. E. Waite, whose contribution to the deck was to give 'instructions', was a member of the Golden Dawn, editor of the magazine *The Unknown World* and called his daughter Sybil (which seems rather on the nose). More surprisingly, he supported his mysticism as a manager for Horlicks, the manufacturer of malted milk. Aleister Crowley referred to him as 'Dead Waite'.

Pamela Colman Smith, who drew the cards, was a much more interesting character. Her projects were numerous and fascinating: she illustrated Jamaican folk tales and Bram Stoker's *The Lair of the White Worm*; did artwork for W. B. Yeats and women's suffrage. Alfred Stieglitz even gave her an exhibition in New York.

You will notice, though, that the deck is called the Rider–Waite not Smith–Waite. Rider after the publishers, Rider Company. Unacknowledged women are easy to forget. The future came. Tastes changed. Life shrank. When Pamela Colman Smith died her possessions were auctioned off to pay her debts, and she was buried in an unmarked grave.

The thing I fear most is diminishment. I used to think that fear was a kind of protection. Like, if Jason came back late after DJ-ing and taking tabs of fuck knows what and I couldn't get through on his phone and imagined him dead then he couldn't be dead, because that would be too much of a coincidence. Or maybe I almost thought it was win–win. Like, if he was dead, at least that would be proof I had supernatural powers, which might be a comfort. But as you get older, more and more of the things you fear happening just happen anyway, and the comfort prescience offers turns out to be very limited.

*

The psychic, of course, is on a screen. It adds to the falsity of the proceedings. The *taroch*; the foolishness. I've waited until Jason is out doing an essential shop at Aldi. He's made Xander go with him for fresh air. My backdrop is the washing-up rack. Hers is a lounge like a showroom: grey and white, fake white roses in a grey vase.

The reader, Rae, has very sleek blonde hair, nail extensions, shiny beige lips like the upholstery on a sports car. Rae pulls out a pack and starts shuffling. 'Would you like to set an intention?' she asks in this girlish voice. Vocal fry.

'Not really,' I say. 'I'm just wondering about the future a lot.'

'Hmm,' she says, beginning to lay cards down. 'You're blessed, but you're also going through a difficult time. You feel unsupported, am I right?'

'I guess,' I say.

'And you're worried about health, about your family's health. I see challenges ahead. I see – does this mean anything to you? I see the letter J.'

'Jason,' I say, taking a gulp of my coffee from my mug that says MAKE ROME GREAT AGAIN with a picture of Nero. Is that the kind of tell cold readers use? 'My husband is called Jason.'

'I see positive things around the letter J. Clarity. Rediscovering yourself.' I feel disappointed when she says that; feel myself swallowing down disappointment. I wonder if she's had Botox. I keep thinking about the money I'm paying her. Fifty pounds. A lot. Not that it's unaffordable, but I never spend that much on myself; always buy clothes from H&M when all my colleagues are in Reiss and COS.

'Okay.'

'Interesting. This card is The World,' Rae says, gesturing down at her spread. 'It's about being centred. Flow. Yours is upside down. You want this reading because you feel stagnant, right, stuck in a rut? You need to find your reason.'

It's true. This part's true at least. 'What, though?' I say.

'I'm sorry,' she says. 'That's your own journey of discovery.'

Of course that's what she says. The banality of it. I find it hard to keep my eyebrow from arching. From giving away some little tell. 'Is that right?'

But then she lays down the final card, what will be – and I see what it is. It's the fucking Nine of Swords. And I suddenly feel a kind of shivering come over me, I'm actually shaking, like I've done something to myself, something irreparable. Because my life is the Ten of Cups and I should have been content and now I can see what I shouldn't see and what I didn't want to see. What a human shouldn't see. That what is coming is failure, despair, death.

Rae must notice I'm paler. 'Well, I mean, it's not a great card,' she says. 'It can mean illness: physical, mental. Great difficulties. It can mean menopause, actually –' she checks to see if I look offended by that – 'But, you know, when I see this I always say to people: you need to ask for help. This year is going to be hard for a lot of folks but, you know, you should talk about it. Don't just lie in bed every night like this poor soul, having migraines and imagining the worst . . .'

I say: 'Sorry, you're buffering, I better go,' and I *leave meeting*.

Haematomancy: Prophecy by Blood

*'I see the disinfectant that knocks it out in a minute, one minute.
And is there a way we can do something like that by injection inside
or almost a cleaning?' the president said during his briefing.*

'You're always on that stupid phone, Mum,' Xander
observes. I put it down and look him in his eyes and try on
a smile.

'You're right. It's just Trump saying we should swallow
bleach to get rid of the virus. Or no, inject bleach into our
blood.'

'I think I'm probably allergic,' he replies, deadpan. He's still
in his Fortnite jamas at eleven. Has he brushed his teeth?

'So this Joe Wicks character, then,' I say, remembering that
fitness guy, over the voices in my head saying: *addiction
unhealthy habits mental health issues.* 'The school reckons we
should . . .'

'Lock him up for crimes against children?'

I chalk this up as me trying but it's really not, it's not even
him trying: both of us half-heartedly reading out the script.

In the afternoon he gets a nosebleed over his pyjamas, which he's still in. I have to tell myself that blood is not an omen. I have to tell myself that as a child I had a lot of nosebleeds. Once, even, actually, I recall having one as a teenager whilst I was snogging this boy in a club and it spilt in his mouth.

Now I have such heavy periods, like I'm pissing blood, since, well, it. Sometimes I use a Mooncup – not instead, as well. The blood in that seems deeper in colour and the smell is very intense, an almost heady broth. Kind of like a meat vermouth. I find the first spots in my pants after I've cleaned up his nose; tell myself that's why I feel so stressed.

That night I lie awake for hours under the nine pale blades.

Jason cuddles me in bed in the morning. It feels unusual, it's been so long, his arms around me in the thin light. I can feel his cock hard against my knickers. 'Sorry, time of the month,' I say.

Postdiction:
Prophecy Written After the Fact

The world, though, the world.

Jason and I drink two bottles of wine whilst we watch the chief advisor to the British Prime Minister, Dominic Cummings, take a press conference in the rose garden. Trump has a rose garden too. It seems they find it an appropriate setting for violent nonsense, like the rose garden in *Alice in Wonderland*. Cummings drove to Durham whilst he thought he had coronavirus, and his excuses are labyrinthian – they seem based on a plausible horror of looking after his own child, but only work if journalists are complicit in the vast, mutual pretence that all the rich people haven't been using nannies from day one, and that he'd be unable to find childcare in London.

There's this preposterous extra bonus lie too, about driving to Barnard Castle to test his eyesight. 'Cunt,' Jason says, topping up his glass, and then he shakes his head in disbelief and laughs a hopeless little laugh.

'Surely everyone can see it now?' I say. 'Surely everyone feels like a mug? I mean, people have missed funerals. There are kids locked up like prisoners who haven't seen another child since –'

'We've been doing the right thing. Xander'll be fine,' Jason says. 'If you're still stressing out about that. He's one of the lucky ones, he's got a computer, a garden.' I bristle when he says this. He's so stubbornly optimistic. If you worry about something in the future he'll bite your head off – *You don't know, do you? So stop being such a miserable bitch. I don't need it.* It's always hard persuading him we need to take Xander to hospital when I see the telltale hives; his eyes glazing. I'm not saying he doesn't love our son as much as I do, but he won't believe the bad thing is actually happening.

I swallow. I swallow words and wine and nine swords.

I pour another glass. The second bottle has gone down so quickly. Cummings is meant to be this super-forecaster. 'For years,' he says in his prepared statement, 'I have warned of the dangers of pandemics. Last year I wrote about the possible threat of coronaviruses and the urgent need for planning.'

But the one mention of coronaviruses on Cummings' blog was added on the 14th of April.

The technical term is 'retroactive clairvoyance' or 'post-diction' or, in the Latin maxim, *vaticinium ex eventu*. Prophecy written after the fact. There is an interesting essay by Lucian on a 'false prophet' of his time, the second century AD, called Alexander of Macedon. It is about, he warns: 'the doings of a person whose deserts entitle him not to be read about by the cultivated, but torn to pieces in an amphitheatre by apes or foxes, with a vast audience looking on.'

Alexander would proclaim that on a stated day a god would give answers. For a price, people could write down what they wished to know and seal it in a packet with wax or clay. After this, he would 'learn' the god's thoughts, then return the packets with their seals intact and the answers attached. In fact, Alexander had various methods of undoing these seals so he could read the questions, make up answers, reseal and return them, to general astonishment. Often, the god's responses prescribed 'cytmide', a goat's fat salve, the name of which was his invention. For predictions about ambitions, he took care never to assign dates, the formula being: 'All this shall come to pass when it is my will.'

Lucian writes: 'It was one of [Alexander's] happiest thoughts to issue prophecies after the event – antidotes to premature utterances which had not been borne out.' Often he promised a sick man would recover before his death, only to claim afterwards that there had been another line: 'No longer seek to arrest thy disease; Thy fate is manifest and inevitable.'

In Rome, he established an intelligence bureau manned with accomplices, who would send him information on people's characters and ambitions, gathering data so that he had his answers ready before the messengers even reached him.

Ultimately, though, his fate was not as he predicted. Alexander had stated, rather optimistically, that he would live to a hundred and fifty then die by a thunderbolt. Before seventy, instead, gangrene inched from foot to crotch; riddled his leg with maggots. 'It was then proved that he was bald, as he was forced by pain to let the doctors make cooling applications to his head, which they could not do without removing his wig.'

Chiromancy:
Prophecy by Palm Reading

I read a think piece that says handshakes are over.

Once a boy read my palm at a party. He wanted to stroke my hand with his finger, I think, that delicate skin where it tickles. It was his schtick, super-forecaster. Little wet teeth flashing; knowing arched eyebrows. I remember very clearly he looked at my lifeline and said with a smile: 'You're going to live longer than you want to.'

Perhaps that's why it doesn't occur to me that the Nine of Swords might mean I catch Covid and die. Lying in bed at night, I rehearse various horrific scenarios: Xander dying, my mum dying, Jason even, but I'm not the one being intubated, it's never me.

Perhaps that's why I've never bothered much with exercise either. Jason starts jogging, muttering something about the couch to 5K, hoping to outrace death. Sometimes I walk to Morrisons or drag Xander on a walk.

Late spring, and the weather is dissonantly joyous. In the park we notice someone is chalking arrows pointing to wild flowers and weeds. Labelling them: alkanet, herb Robert, celandine. I tell myself it's a generous thing to do, but I feel this weird, low-grade anger, like every single petty thing in the world is now becoming an Instagram opportunity; is demanding my attention.

The countryside and beaches begin to fill with people who don't normally go to the countryside and beaches. They're even swimming in London's filthy canals. Touching everything. Our early communal dream that Covid-19 might make the world purer, the air brighter, is exposed as wilful blindness. The pictures of dolphins in Venetian canals or whatever have gone. Now the news shows photos of used toilet roll, disposable gloves and dirty nappies. Beer cans. Pale-blue masks bloating in puddles of piss.

A uniformed cleaner in the park tells me: 'Watch out, love, there's human shit literally everywhere.'

Zoomancy:
Prophecy by Animal Behaviour

The plague summer passes quickly at first, as we gain some incremental freedoms.

There is a sense of liberation in the air after Edward Colston's statue topples. Jason organizes a couple of BBQs with friends in our garden, where he teaches Xander to make ribs and use a kitchen knife; plays Balearic beats through the Bluetooth. He's one of those clichéd men who only cook over fire. There are piles of charred meat and bones left over afterwards, as if we've entertained the crew of the *Argo*.

Another weekend, we have a picnic with his sister, Sophie, and her family, who bring their own cups and tubs of elaborately delicious salads we're not allowed to eat and lay out their rugs at exactly two metres away. In the parks of South-East London there are always feral green parakeets. Somehow I find myself telling Sophie's glazed face about the parrot astrologers of Tamil Nadu who are trained to pick fortune cards. 'A bit like that psychic octopus, Paul, you know, who could predict the World Cup results,' I say, as she passive-aggressively tops up her own Prosecco.

Xander goes to the football cage with his friends a dozen times, even though that girl was stabbed in the back in a London park by a boy who never said a word as part of a gang initiation. But home-school has finished; he needs company. I tell him he can't wear his good trainers. *He'll be fine*, Jason says. *He needs fresh air. To mess around with a ball and other lads. He's got to grow up.* I wonder if Jason thinks being white is some kind of inoculation. We decide Jaden's the responsible one so teach him how to use an EpiPen. When Xander's out I just empty my mind as though I don't have a child.

Jason's friends are still having crises. Meesha dumps Toby, and I have to pretend I don't think it's absolutely the right decision. Meanwhile, Joey's furloughed and is apparently dabbling in crack, because the lockdown has caused a nationwide cocaine drought. He gets himself banned from his local pub; causes a kitchen fire.

Our family of three go for a trip to the zoo, though, one day, when it's allowed to open. That's a happy day. We suck ice pops. Xander loves the tiger, its shoulder blades rolling as it paces by the glass. The lockdown has been terrible for zoos. The animals still need feeding: thousands of cucumbers and melons; box after box of fish; endless frozen mice; a parade of goat carcasses. I sympathize with the keepers, in their green bodywarmers, as they shovel hay into baskets. All that care and no one to witness. I tell Jason and Xander how, after the Prussian siege, residents of Paris had to eat the zoo animals. Victor

Hugo ate elephant steak. 'Great fact, Mum,' Xander smiles, thumbs-upping me. Since home-school started, he likes to tease me about my great facts.

Pretty much everything is labelled endangered. Jason is the family photographer – he's got the best camera on his phone – although I don't think he's ever taken a picture of me where I don't look like shit. When he's not picking up a work call, he takes lots of photos of me and Xander smiling in front of cages that I wish he'd delete.

Oneiromancy: Prophecy by Dreams

The light is very clear at summer solstice. In my garden, orange nasturtiums; lavender. The gorse bush that the previous owner planted smells of honey. Inside, Xander is in the darkened living room, watching a movie with the curtains drawn; that squidgy distractor toy pulsing in his hand. 'You should come outside, it's lovely,' I shout at him, sitting with my coffee and my yoghurt at the garden table, feeling not bad, actually. I close my eyes and lift them. Kaleidoscopic pink.

Once, when I was a girl, I put seven wild flowers under my pillow at midsummer; I think my best friend, Nicola, told me to. I can still picture them, bruised and flattened on the sheet. I was supposed to dream of my true love but I didn't dream of anything.

Instagram is getting better at pre-empting my desires: trousers that aren't short on the ankle; book-length lyrical essays; pretty cotton face masks. The cool younger literary women on the platform burn sage and make solstice tinctures of petals in shallow bowls and I wish I was that kind of person, less self-conscious. But then I'm never sure whether those women mean it. I mean, they lay out these beautiful tarot spreads on blankets but I don't think they believe in the supernatural. They just lay out little shrines to themselves; create these rituals in order to be able to think about themselves more profoundly for longer.

Still, I like the aesthetic. They all follow this publisher, Ignota, who have a countdown clock on their website until Capricorn moves into Aquarius on the 17th of December, completing a three-year arc of ordeal and challenge, and we enter a new Air Era. I click on it and end up buying a book, then clicking on other pages and ordering a translation of the I Ching that comes with fifty hand-picked yarrow sticks, and also a jar of lucid dreaming tablets. Afterwards, I feel like a bit of a prick, but it's research, I tell myself, the impact of ancient divination methods on our present-day modes of premonition, from astrology apps to surveillance capitalism predicting our buying habits. Blah blah.

Apparently lucid dreaming in lockdown is a thing. Twitter is full of it. Professional dream analysts say, 'The more intense and bizarre the dream, the more likely you are to remember it, and stressful times mean stressful dreams [. . .] dream recall is also easier when you can linger under the duvet and have time to replay it, instead of racing off to your commute.'

When I was young I had a dream dictionary. What happened to it? The Ancient Sumerians had Dream Priests. The Egyptians had their Dream Book. The Greeks believed gods communicated with mortals through dreams. Penelope dreams of fifty geese killed by an eagle, and then Odysseus returns and kills the suitors. In the second century AD, Artemidorus, a Greek physician who lived in Rome, wrote that there were two classes of dreams: the *somnium*, which forecast events, and the *insomnium*, which are concerned with present matters. His *Oneirocritica* (Interpretation of Dreams) is a dream dictionary. Within it, Artemidorus tells us that dreams of having sex with your mother can admit many interpretations, and it depends very much on the sexual position.

Every day more padded envelopes arrive at our house. Plastic packages. Amazon boxes, that swoosh on the side like a self-satisfied smirk. The lucid dreaming tablets come first. The jar talks about Oneironautics, from the Greek words *oneira*, meaning 'dream', and *nautis*, meaning 'sailor'. *An oneironaut is someone who has learned to travel consciously in the dream world.* There are thirty blue pills and thirty red ones. The blue ones contain 5-Hydroxytryptophan and mugwort, and increase the time spent in REM sleep. The red ones contain Huperzine-A and choline, and aid dream memory and rational thinking during sleep.

I take a red pill three hours before, then a blue one at bedtime. But in the first dream I don't travel. I don't have any control. In the dream I am in a prison cell, and I feel very, very powerless. My crime is a translation. I know nothing I can say will get me out if they want me in there. I write this down in a little notebook by the bed, and feel sad and small.

The next night I dream our house is on fire, only when I run to the window it is not just our house but every house on our street, every house in the whole city, and London is burning down like Troy. Or no, something much closer. Like the Californian coast. Like the Blue Mountains. Like the Amazon rainforest. Like somewhere now.

This is a lucid dream, I think. *I can control it. I can stop the fire.*

But I just stand there without any idea how.

Causimancy: Prophecy by Burning

No Roman sacred objects were guarded as carefully as the Sibylline Books, which were said to contain fragments of oracular prophecies.

According to tradition, they were bought from the Sibyl at Cumae by the last king of Rome, Tarquin the Proud. She offered Tarquin nine books of these prophecies, but he insisted that the price was too high, and so she burned three and offered the remaining six to him at the same price. Again Tarquin refused, so the Sibyl burned three more and once again repeated her offer. It was only then that he relented, purchasing the last three at the full original price.

From then on, the Sibylline Books were stored in a vault beneath the Capitoline Temple of Jupiter, where they were consulted at momentous crises throughout the Republic's history. The Romans, for example, leafed hurriedly through them after Hannibal annihilated their troops at Cannae, and on their 'recommendation', two Gauls and two Greeks were buried alive. They were consulted when stones rained from the sky, when the day went dark, in times of plague. Nero consulted them after the fire. There are various theories as to what happened to them. It is most often said that the Sibylline Books were destroyed by the general Flavius Stilicho, as they were being used to attack his government.

The security of the Sibylline Books was important, as their dire and ambiguous predictions could lead to political instability, much like the leaks of Covid-19 modelling or advice from the Scientific Advisory Group for Emergencies (SAGE).

Hydatomancy: Prophecy by Rainwater

Once we're legally permitted, I go to see my mum for the day. I feel obliged. I set off at dawn and drive all the way to Barnsley with Xander – it takes four hours, listening to the penultimate *Harry Potter* as an audiobook, the rain getting heavier the whole way – and then sit in her yard at two metres' distance whilst she dunks a biscuit in her tea. 'I'd offer you one,' she says, 'but no point not being careful.' Her mouth has deep lines scored around it; is wet and red inside like the mouth of a volcano. At least she isn't in a care home with a 'hug room'. I'd have to hug her even more awkwardly than usual through a transparent plastic sheet.

She's actually in a bad mood because she touched the bin this morning then forgot to wash her hands straight away, the implication being it's my fault for visiting. 'Jean from club can't walk on her own any more,' she says. 'Long Covid. It's terrible. And all these youngsters having parties.' I ask if she's witnessed these parties but she just complains the young ones on her road haven't knocked on her door or offered help, not even that lad who brought the sandbags when the floods came.

Xander asks about the floods, and she shrugs. Xander says: 'By the time I'm Mum's age the whole of Hull will be underwater.'

I can't wait to drive home. Honestly. My main takeaway is she got an Asda delivery slot in the end but it took her hours and then they'd swapped out her shortcrust pastry for filo pastry and her egg custards for tinned custard.

*

They furloughed half the staff, because it's free money – they'd be mugs not to – but then expect Jason to basically do a second job for the same wage. Redundancies are coming, everyone knows it. This is the stated reason why Jason can't drive to Barnsley with us. Every night he sits at the kitchen table working on his laptop whilst watching box sets I've signalled my indifference to.

He misses the commute, I think, podcasts and a flat white, the little treats that capitalism doles out every time you hit the button.

When we get home he isn't there. Xander goes back on the computer (almost a day without it, God). And then I get a text, *work meeting has carried on to the pub*, and that night he still isn't back.

At one I wake and get a cold feeling of premonition, of something wrong. I can hear rain on the roof. I run downstairs and fling the front door open and he's slumped on the step with no socks on. On the dirty soggy little shoe mat. Drunk old man like my father. A cut; something trickling and spreading. Ugly.

I'm sure I can smell piss. I want to hit him so hard.

My next thought is Xander. I don't want him to see his dad like this. I drag Jason's body like a corpse over the threshold. 'Get up,' I hiss. 'Upstairs, now,' like I might hiss to Xander. *Go to your room.* And I kind of push Jason up the first steep step and then he trips up the set of them like a sacrificial goat up to the altar.

Oinomancy: Prophecy by Wine

In the morning when I get into the kitchen he is chewing.

The golden fur on his soft pink chin is like that on a very unappealing peach. Is there anything worse than a man in a dressing gown? Thin hairy calves poking out. I have to spend the rest of my life with this. I promised.

'What?' he says. 'I couldn't find my key, okay? I didn't want to wake you and Xander up.'

'Like you remember.'

'I just did, right? You found me on the doorstep.'

'*Slumped!*' I whisper-shout, thinking of Xander; the neighbours whose own rows we hear word for word. '*You were fucking unconscious.*'

'I wasn't, actually, I was just taking a moment to think, okay? Look, I haven't been out since lockdown. I drank too much, that's all, we all do at the moment. It's just – pressure. Unconscious! Pull your fucking horns in, honestly. You've been getting through the wine quick enough yourself most nights.' He tries to slip a hand around my waist, as if it might appease me, but I squirm away.

*

I've not mentioned Trump much but he's always there, leering over us. Standing in front of a church, holding a Bible, after protesters demonstrating against racism have been aggressively cleared from the area. Retweeting a video in which someone yells 'White power'. Suggesting his administration should test coronavirus less. Every day he finds some way to be the news. I read this astonishing book of poetry during lockdown, *Vertigo & Ghost*, by Fiona Benson, after a colleague recommends it, and her Zeus is an unrepentant filthy rapist who speaks only in capitals: '*HEY HONEYS / I'M HOME*.' I can't help thinking of Benson's Zeus every time I see Trump. Her Zeus who 'can walk between raindrops / without getting wet'.

It amazes me how, even though I've read all 705 pages of Shoshana Zuboff's *The Age of Surveillance Capitalism* and was completely convinced by it, when Twitter nudges me towards some opinion piece on Trump on some news site, I can't consent to all the cookies quickly enough. Take all the data you want so long as you get that box of text out of my way. This is how the world ends, isn't it?

Someone pressing:

I agree   I agree   I agree   I agree

*

I dream about the prison cell again. The government have special powers now. They can arrest you for anything if they want. Casual sex. A children's birthday party.

Still, when Jason's dad asks us over for lunch he's there with his long-term girlfriend and about fifteen other people on the decking, pink short sleeves rolled up, silver fox. 'Well, nearly my birthday, so.' That self-satisfied smile. He pours Chablis, mentions his friend who works at the *Spectator*; how he's flying out next week to his favourite little spot in Palma. He never even thought he should let us know it would be a gathering. He never thinks the rules apply to him. Perhaps they don't.

Phrenology: Prophecy by the Configuration of the Brain

I get my hair cut. I lean back over the sink, the shudder of its porcelain against my neck, her hands caught in my foaming hair, and tell myself: *try to enjoy this*. It's hard though, I'm mainly thinking about whether we should ban Xander from WhatsApp because according to Jaden's mum there's been bullying, although Xander and Jaden didn't join in, just watched. Also, Tyler shared a picture of his girlfriend in her sports bra, next to another radiator.

When I get home we've become the owners of a phrenology head. I'd rather have a palmistry palm, but it's a gift of sorts. Jason lent money to Joey knowing he probably shouldn't, and he didn't pay him back but now we get this head I assume he bought during some crack session. One of those gestures we make to feel spontaneous that don't quite work because they're gestures.

The head is a pale, dingy grey with that crazed crackle glaze, and there is a kind of corridor down the middle of the skull with all these rectangles coming off it, like it's a map of a university department. It's notable how some qualities just have a tiny one-centimetre square on the forehead – like reason – but then domestic propensities has this whole great chunk of head, really half the back. Selfish sentiments too. Like nearly an eighth of the skull.

Scrying: Prophecy by Gazing

Outside of term I'm meant to be working on a translation. I was meant to be working on the translation of a second novel, actually, that I preferred, having put loads of effort into the sample chapters, but those publishers decided to stop acquiring new translations because of Covid. My income is definitely withering – panels cancelled, an essay, a talk – though I haven't felt it much because I've spent so much less.

Anyway, this German novel is based on the Faust myth. The novelist doesn't speak very good English; she seems happy with me doing what I like. Work for me currently means sitting at the kitchen table getting through two cafetières of coffee by myself. After the first cup I microwave the subsequent ones until the mug has a dirty ring. I'm used to the constant churn of the washing machine; the gurgle of the dishwasher. Jason has the study and he's always on a conference call, trying to massage the egos of interchangeable men. Xander's mainly summering in the living room or his room. Sometimes I hear Jason shout something at him like *practise your drums* or *don't practise your drums*.

I can see why the novelist decided to update the Faust legend. Faust wants magic powers with which to indulge all the pleasure and knowledge of the world. In return he makes a bargain with the devil's representative, Mephistopheles, to be permanently enslaved. We have all made that pact, now. In our phones, those little black mirrors, we stare and scry into the glass all day. There our every dream or whim can materialize: we can find every song or movie from history; every niche of porn; maps of all the world; forecasts; casinos; galleries; celebrities eating breakfast; sporting victories; snuff. We can view every street and see real-time footage of polar bear cubs or war zones. We are like Goethe's Faust declaring:

> Whatever is permitted humankind
> I want to taste it deep within myself.
> I want to grasp what's high, sink into low,
> to pile each grief and bliss up in my breast,
> expanding this sole self titanically.

But in exchange for this we have sold ourselves. Like Faust, we are the product.

[Pause whilst I check out my twelve WhatsApp notifications.]

Inevitably, I find myself researching variants of the Faust legend, falling down Wikipedia holes. Indulging in all the knowledge of the world. The legend began in Germany with the historical Johann Georg Faust (1480–1540), a performer of magic tricks and horoscopes. The Latin adjective *faustus* means 'lucky' or 'auspicious'. Christopher

Marlowe's Doctor Faustus may have been influenced by John Dee, an Anglo-Welsh mathematician, occultist and alchemist who was the court astronomer for, and advisor to, Elizabeth I. A long beard white as milk. As a political advisor, he advocated for the founding of English colonies in the New World to form a 'British Empire', a term he coined.

Dee claimed that angels dictated several books to him through a scryer or crystal-gazer called Kelley, in the 'Language of Angels' or 'Adamical Language' because, according to Dee's Angels, Adam used it in Paradise to name all things. The letters are read from right to left.

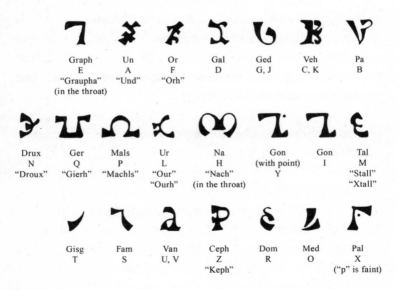

Graph	Un	Or	Gal	Ged	Veh	Pa
E	A	F	D	G, J	C, K	B
"Graupha"	"Und"	"Orh"				
(in the throat)						

Drux	Ger	Mals	Ur	Na	Gon	Gon	Tal
N	Q	P	L	H	(with point)	I	M
"Droux"	"Gierh"	"Machls"	"Our"	"Nach"	Y		"Stall"
			"Ourh"	(in the throat)			"Xtall"

Gisg	Fam	Van	Ceph	Dom	Med	Pal
T	S	U, V	Z	R	O	X
			"Keph"			("p" is faint)

I pore over it one late night after the best part of a bottle.
I'm a linguist. A foolish thought clouds my mind: if I can
learn the language of angels, of Adam . . .

But then I read how Dee's first wife died. His second wife
died. When Dee married his third, his scryer, Kelley, said
the angels wished for them to share their wives. Dee
protested, afraid he was 'pawning his soul', but reply came
that 'Nothing is unlawful which is lawful unto God.' So
they did.

Not the language of angels, then, the language of Mephistopheles. As it all is perhaps: astrology, palmistry. A con
man's language. A code devised for corruption.

Dee returned to Mortlake after six years abroad to find his
home vandalized, his library ruined, his prized books and
instruments stolen. His third wife died of the bubonic
plague. I see it everywhere now, the word 'plague', but
perhaps it was always everywhere.

[Pause to check the *Guardian* UK Coronavirus livestream.]

Urticariaomancy: Prophecy by Itches

Perhaps Jason would wife-swap?

No.

But who am I to have an affair with? How do I have the opportunity, when I don't leave the house? Is sex outside your bubble even legal this week? It's just after my period, when I always feel horny, and I speculate idly, aware of my cunt under my dress, this stupid hunger to fuck before I'm an old crone, but it's impossible; so many kinds of impossible. *Nothing will ever happen again.*

I don't ever think about the possibility of Jason having an affair. I don't know why. If the thought crosses my mind, I just dismiss it in a moment, like junk mail.

When night comes I try to make an effort. Jason gets limp before we finish, mutters apologies – tiredness, the beer – but I take him in my mouth, make him cum.

'We used to have such fun in summer,' he says afterwards. 'Didn't we? That year in Berlin. Festivals every week. We had such a fucking laugh, didn't we?' And he's right. He was doing well as a DJ, before he gave it up when we chose to have Xander, for stability. Before he sold hundreds of his records off in some grand gesture. It seems so far away now it's unreal; it's a shock to think of him thinking of it. *Everything that separates man from man gave way.* Indestructible joy and power; the pouring crowd; his glistening face; him lifting me up; the taste of the sweat of his lips. Coming down on beaches or in the hot caves of tents, where he'd wake with a hard-on. In the Nietzschean divide between the Dionysian and the Apollonian, in our twenties we were very much Team Dionysus although it always worried me a bit, how off my face I needed to get before my brain would let me switch off and enjoy the moment.

'Ugh,' he says. 'Fucking 2020. It'll be fun again though. Next year. We should have some proper fun again.' It sounds so unlikely I feel tenderly towards him, kiss his neck.

*

One morning, when I am washing up, a thought suddenly occurs to me: *I could be on my own for a minute.* A wave of desire.

'Would you look after Xander for half an hour?' I say to Jason, trying to sound casual.

'Of course,' he nods, like it's that easy. 'I'll play computer games with him. Budge up, Xander,' and he picks up the second controller. Xander scratches his wrist and smiles.

'You're toast.'

Why haven't I done this sooner? I don't think it even occurred to me. I shove EpiPens and medicine in Jason's direction, and walk out into sun.

When I get to the end of the road I feel light-headed but also foolish. There's almost nothing I can do to justify this freedom. And it isn't fair on Xander, it looks like I want to escape him. I want to buy an adult drink, something bitter with Campari in it that might flick a switch in my head, but I haven't brought a book out with me. I can't just sit there scrolling through my phone. Instead I walk towards the high street. Non-essential shops are open again. I pull on my mask, dirty from crumbs and pens at the bottom of my handbag, go into a shop and buy a pair of striped socks and a nice-smelling candle that will do for someone.

I bump into a mum, one of Xander's classmate's mums, outside the shop where you refill your washing-up liquid. She has a string bag full of jars. I realize in panic I can't remember her name. 'How's Xander?' she asks.

'You know, managing,' I say. 'How's –' I realize I don't know the name of her children either. 'Your kids,' I say. Thank God they're definitely plural.

'We were lucky,' she says. 'They had a place, my husband's a civil servant so counts as a keyworker. Summer's harder actually, Milo's been driving his brother mad, but we've got a new au pair starting next week.' I haven't missed small talk. Au pair. Fuck her. I'm never going to learn this bitch's name.

*

I'm with Xander in the park, weaving past the cars pulsing exhaust, through the picnic rugs, his cap brim low, his dark clothes absorbing the sunlight. He'll only wear long sleeves this summer – some new self-consciousness. He touches a lamp post. He touches a tree. He touches a gate. The ice-cream van mocks him, arriving with its toxic jingle. He climbs the big climbing frame and comes down the zip wire. He itches the back of his neck. I check my phone and the Duolingo owl is admonishing me for missing a day. Do I want to purchase a streak freeze? I look up and Xander touches his lips. 'Here,' I say, when he's in earshot and I can't bear it any more, holding out a tiny bottle of sanitizer. I'm no longer sure whether it's the Covid germs or just the traces of sesame, and society has normalized my paranoia.

Rub your hands together gently. Be sure to cover the surfaces of both of your hands, including fingers and around your fingertips and nails. You should also rub in the sanitizer about 2 inches (0.051 m) up each wrist.

He's always singing this song 'Dumb Ways to Die'. It's Australian, a railway safety thing – you know, a little video about pastel blobs getting eaten by sharks or putting their fingers in a plug, with this faux-upbeat tune – but I find it hard to breathe when he sings it, let alone put on my patient smile. *So many dumb ways to die.* The clouds are low and dark. Some days I feel like I'm holding up the sky.

When we get home I cook him meat. I feel bad about picnics and ice cream, but meat's okay, he can have meat, I won't allow myself to think about global warming or cancer for now, I put them aside because he deserves a treat; make too much bacon for his lunch exactly as a bad mother might if she did the same thing with different motivations.

Schematomancy: Prophecy by Face

Everyone I follow on social media is very pro-mask, and I am too – I mean, we should all definitely wear one, even though I'm sure my barely washed cotton one doesn't protect me, if only as a basic courtesy to cashiers and bus drivers – but at the same time I hate them. Even if I just wear one for a few minutes, breathing in my own seam of hot, stale air, I feel deeply hassled and impaired, as though I somehow can't see as clearly or hear as well, though neither of those facts can be true.

My colleague Jay's still shielding. They say they haven't left the house since March, which actually sounds to me like it's becoming a mental health issue, though they suffered from Chronic Fatigue Syndrome when they were younger, so I can understand they're afraid of the overlap with Long Covid.

We WhatsApp about YouTube videos, sometimes, or share Classics memes. A woman carves a watermelon into the Colosseum. We both love Emily Wilson, the first female translator of *The Odyssey*, and she starts doing these crazy brilliant Odyssey-a-day videos, reading bits out loud with homemade costumes. Her siren has feathers in her hair and a microphone. Jay uses the word 'stan' and I have to look it up. I follow Jay on Twitter too and they retweet the Anne Carson bot *a lot*. Antigone, particularly, seems a favourite, that young activist eternally defying the boomers. I RT Jay's RTs, or reply with other quotes or emojis: heart emoji, fire emoji, lightning emoji, comedy and tragedy mask emoji. That kind of level of serious academic discussion.

Jay follows @poetastrologers so I follow them too. I remember, the first time I met Jay, they said, 'Don't tell me, you're Libra on the cusp of Scorpio,' and I felt very seen. That's the trick, isn't it? You don't even have to see the right thing, people are just so thrilled you're looking.

Maybe that's why I hate these face masks as well. No one really looks at anyone any more. But no, that's not exactly true – I used to actively enjoy the feeling of anonymity in a city, when anonymity was an opportunity for rebellion or adventure. It's the sense of anonymously conforming I find so precisely grotesque, as though I'm consenting to my own erasure.

Selenomancy: Prophecy by Moon

It's satisfying, when something is named and so illumin-
ated. I am delighted to find there is a German word,
mittelschmerz, for the bitter, grasping pains I've started getting in the middle of my cycle around ovulation.

The moon, though. Tonight I just looked at it. The moon
Homer looked at; Sappho.

It always stuns me.

Silvery, rosy-fingered moon moon moon.

Thriae: Prophecy by Mantic Pebbles

The Ancient World is full of triads. The Furies, of course. The Fates. The Three Graces. The Gorgons. The Graeae, those 'Grey Ones' Xander used to want to hear about as a child, delighted and revolted as the witches pushed one eyeball and greasy yellowed tooth between them.

I've never been part of a girl gang. I could meet other women for a drink now, legally, but no one asks me to. I wasn't very good at maintaining my friendships after I had Xander and then the miscarriage. There's a couple of Oxford Classics friends but one's shielding; the other one's moved out to her mum's second home in Sussex for the summer.

I've always found groups of women intimidating anyway. I read about a triad of sisters called the Thriae, with heads like aged women's, besprinkled as if with white pollen, and the lower bodies and wings of bees, and I think that's how I imagine all women: buzzing with gossip, nectar-eaters, swarming, the potential to sting. They were nymphs of the springs of the Corycian Cave of Mount Parnassus. Pan's cave. I wanted to see it on our Delphi trip. We were meant to see it this year. Would I have felt those monstrous women vibrating in the air: their striped, swollen pelvises; their rapid, translucent wings?

A bee on my sill. I panic. *Xander.*

The bee was believed to be a sacred insect that moved between the natural world and the underworld. Perhaps because a sting can kill – well, those allergic anyway. The Thriae had the power of divination or speaking truth; they aided Apollo in developing his powers. They're associated with telling fortunes by throwing pebbles into an urn. Melaina, one of the Thriae, whose name means 'the black', was perhaps loved by Apollo. In one version of the story she had a child with him called Delphos, from whom Delphi derives its name. The Delphic priestess was often referred to as a 'bee'.

The bee lifts like a tiny drone over a village.

Is that where the name 'drone' comes from? It skitters around like bad luck. Silently, I empty my water glass then slowly slowly creep towards it, sick with concentration.

'What are you doing, Mum?' Xander asks.

'Nothing . . .'   bᴢᴢᴢᴢᴢᴢᴢᴢᴢᴢᴢᴢᴢᴢᴢᴢᴢᴢᴢᴢᴢᴢᴢᴢᴢᴢᴢᴢᴢᴢᴢᴢᴢᴢ

                                                 ᴢ

                                    ᴢ

                              ᴢ

                        ᴢ

                  ᴢᴢᴢᴢᴢᴢᴢᴢᴢᴢᴢᴢᴢᴢᴢᴢᴢᴢᴢᴢᴢᴢᴢᴢᴢᴢttttt
                  SLAM [⁻.] 'Got it!'

She rattles inside like a pebble, butting against the urn's ceiling. Prophetic. Endangered. Unstrokeable fur. To defend herself is to kill herself, her body a trick or a trap.

'Poor bee,' Xander says. 'We're supposed to save the bees, Mum.' But I haven't harmed it, have I? It's still alive. *I'm saving you*, I think. *I think I'm saving you.*

Alphitomancy: Prophecy by Barley

Has this month been a blink or endless? I think a lot about time. Aristotle believed that if nothing changes, then time doesn't pass. Time is our way of situating ourselves in relation to change.

Once, when I was always on the bus and actually had time to read for pleasure, I read Carlo Rovelli's *Order of Time*. I was struck by the idea that 'things' – a stone, a tree – are actually better understood as monotonous events.

This summer, I feel like a monotonous event.

When I read the Greek myths I always have this sense that life is like a computer game to them. That sounds stupid, but I mean – when Dido kills herself or the cave door rolls shut on Antigone I imagine a sign flashing up like GAME OVER GAME OVER. There's the Olympian board game in the *Jason and the Argonauts* movie, I guess. That idea of us as living pawns, which we are. But it's definitely a computer game that I think of.

The many-worlds interpretation (MWI) of quantum physics suggests that we live in a near-infinity of universes.

Every decision we make splits us into multiple copies. In many of these universes there are replicas of ourselves, leading other lives. My other selves with their different lovers, their breathing daughters, their living fathers, their dead sons. Their many, many dead sons. I pity those last poor cows for their minor missteps: that hesitation to call an ambulance, that misread label, that crumb. I picture them killing themselves, putting themselves out of their misery. GAME OVER GAME OVER.

If I was capable of writing novels, I'd write a novel about a man who is always his luckiest self – who has the knack, somehow, of sliding into the right world with every accident; every decision. A man who has everything, wins everything, but has to live with the guilt of leaving his thousand other selves to suffer, lose, die; scattered through time and space, cursing him.

*

Maybe in the future this will all just be a game.

People want that, don't they? They're called Accelerationists. They want computer technology sped up and intensified – because it's for the best, and there's no alternative anyway. They want total automation. They want the digital and the human to merge. They call that the Singularity – the digital and human becoming one, so we can leave this grubby, material world behind.

Or there are Patternists who, similarly, view consciousness as a persisting pattern of matter and energy. These
patterns, which contain our identity, currently run on the
body – a dated piece of physical hardware. But they
believe that in the future these patterns will be transferred
into robots; downloaded into supercomputers. Our souls
will become immortal, our bodies irrelevant.

I tried out Virtual Reality for the first time a while ago,
quite randomly, in the Tate Modern. It was Modigliani's
studio. Dim and small, the rain pissing down the windows.
And I couldn't hold it in my head that I was in a room in
the Tate Modern and in Modigliani's studio at the same
time, I couldn't process it.

Another time it was at a university, in a seminar room, and
with the headset on I stood waist high in a field of quivering corn and there was some brute monument in it, some
hulking grey standing stone, and I was there but not, and
I thought about my son so far away and felt an awful sor-
row, like I knew he would end up in this place and I missed
his stooped scratchy body already.

In the actual future we will escape there, or no, we will
be herded there to keep us occupied, producing data
instead of revolution, taking up minimal resources. If
we are in there we will soon forget we are actually somewhere else too, a depleted world, shrinking, saline,
poisonous.

One night, after a lucid dreaming pill, I have another pre-monition. It is very clear and true. In the actual future I am in a field of barley, waist high, poppies, a tiny mouse coiled, wild flowers, a rainbow, a scudding cirrus, except this is VR and I cannot feel the warmth of the grain between my fingers or smell anything and there is something about the dragonfly which skids past that is not exactly right, I'm sure, some tiny lack.

There is always this dull pressure around my eyes.

I am always speaking to Xander but I am not wholly sure he is my son, is he my son? I know Xander would be the first to move into that world, careless of his flesh and bone. He would trade his real skin gladly for those 'skins' he trades in.

But in the future there is no moisture on his breath, no sweat on his lip, some tiny lack. A carelessness in the design. His hands, his hands are smooth. And I start to become convinced it isn't him. It's a trick, he's not there, it isn't actually him. What have they done with him?

I am always living in someone else's thoughts, and maybe this is just who he thinks my son is and not my son.

*

Many religious people believe the world is full of signs. That we can read it. The car is meant to crash, the street

to flood, the marriage to be tested, the cancer to dupli-
cate, the baby to die. Each is a punishment or test or
blessing. The Ancient Greeks believed every comet was a
sign, every thunderbolt, every piece of meat. Everything
was riddled with signs. Infested. Writers transmute the
world into signs, they make a world that's orderly and
holy; in the novels I translate, everything means something and is put there just so: the barley, the rain, the lilac
ball gown, the eczema. Some people see the real world
like this – they think that the graffiti that says TIGGER is a
message, the cereal packet is a message, red vans are
code – and we call them mad. But in the actual future the
VR world we exist in really will indeed be readable. The
wallflower, the cancer, the tag, the worm, the brand of
crisps, the colour of his shirt. I mean, it will actually be
written in code, and when we interpret it like a dream or a
story full of symbols, that is what it will be.

Gyromancy: Prophecy by Dizziness

When I walk into the study to get the ironing bag and Jason's playing Candy Crush, I actually almost spin out with fury.

Candy Crush Gate.

I take a breath and try to parse my reaction in the moment, before I speak, and I think about how I managed to get Xander into a summer art club that day that wasn't fully booked or cancelled and could deal with his allergies, had to fill in all these forms with his details, to make his packed lunch and drive him fifteen minutes to drop him off at 9.45, then drive back for a Zoom tutorial with this pain-in-the-arse PhD student who constantly hounds me, barely got a couple of hours on my translation, then had to drive back out to pick Xander up at 3.15 and admire some cereal boxes that had undergone, frankly, the bare minimum of intervention, drive back via Tesco and the garage, make Xander's tea then prep ours, play football with him in the garden, wash up – okay, I'm boring myself now – and am about to do the ironing whilst Xander is finally allowed his screen time, which I feel guilty about, and all day Jason has been in the study because he has 'so much work on' and it turns out he's playing this most pathetic little mindless opiate game, lining up plasticky 'sweets' that look like the kind of jewellery you give a three-year-old.

'What?' he asks.

'Nothing,' I say. 'What are you playing?'

'Candy Crush Saga.'

'Saga? As in a long and complex narrative, possibly written in Old Norse?'

'I just needed five minutes, I had a really shit call. A funding partner's pulling out. I think I'm allowed a five-minute break, I don't work in an Amazon warehouse.'

'Oh,' I say. 'Sorry. I had a shit call today too.'

'*Yes*,' he exclaims, as a little line of candies disappears, signalling the conversation is over. I take the ironing downstairs. I realize that if Jason had an affair I would be able to forgive the sex but I would never ever be able to forgive him the time.

*

What if this is all a game?

There was an article in the *Guardian* once, by Meghan O'Gieblyn, about a type of faith called transhumanism, where she noted that the word 'transhuman' first appears in Henry Francis Cary's 1814 translation of Dante's 'Paradiso', the last book of the *Divine Comedy*. Dante is ascending into the spheres of heaven when his human flesh is transformed. 'Words may not tell of that transhuman change.'

She writes of the belief that God is the designer and Jesus his digital avatar. That the Christian belief in the Rapture, the end time when Christians will leave their fleshy bodies behind and rise 'in the clouds, to meet the Lord in the air', has many parallels with the concept of the Singularity. That moment our souls become immortal, forever and ever amen.

Rapture is from the Latin *raptus*, to be 'seized'. The same root as raptor or rape. That human wish to be overpowered; subsumed.

What if this is VR already? I start to think about it often. I read how Elon Musk thinks we are in a simulation. I heard him talk about it once – how if some disaster doesn't erase civilization, then technological progress means simulations indistinguishable from reality are inevitable. And if that's the case, we're probably in one. We should basically hope we're in one.

When I drink more than a bottle and close my eyes in bed and can't stop the spinning, the gyring dark, I feel almost as though my mind is part of an enormous network stretching through the infinite blackness, connected by a million tiny flickering connections, like interlaced, spinning snowflakes. Are the granular 'quanta', the grains of the universe, a sort of pixel?

The many-worlds theory is based on the observer effect, which says that the attempt to observe something causes it to change. The smaller the object, the truer this is. Like when you look at something with your VR headset on and it recognizes you have held your gaze and the door opens.

Midnight. *1.18*. I touch my phone and its lit face tells the time: *2.26*. A sip of water. The longer I lie dizzy and sleepless in bed the more I think this is a game. Is it a multiplayer game? Is the purpose of the game to save the world? To be good? I read that human life on earth could end in fifty years, about when my own life might be expected to end. Can that be a coincidence? All my childhood history lessons were about the Nazis and asking what we would have done, and now fascism is happening again. Is that a coincidence?

If this is all a test, this game I am playing, then what is the aim of it? To experience all I can? But I'm just in this house, day in, day out. I am failing terribly at this game. I have got myself stuck on this one crappy level. What do I need to do to move on to the next level?

Papyromancy:
Prophecy by Paper Money

Some people can escape this crappy level. Some people appear, suddenly, to have materialized in France or Spain or Greece, posting pictures from sandy coves. *Seem to have found ourselves in Puglia!* Especially rich people. The subject of Delphi comes up again, but we still haven't got a voucher or a refund for our last flights, and Jason can't take time off. *Next spring* we promise Xander, like the promises of adults or travel agencies mean anything any more.

I keep thinking about going there, though. Fantasizing. The first sanctuary at Delphi was made of beeswax and feathers; the second of ferns; the third of laurel; the fourth of bronze with golden nightingales on the roof (but the earth engulfed it); the fifth of stone (which burned down), before it was replaced with the present shrine.

The Temple of Apollo has 147 maxims inscribed on it, said to come from the Pythia, and so from Apollo. The three most famous are carved above the entrance:

Know thyself

Nothing in excess

Surety brings ruin

Cybermancy: Prophecy by Computer

Sehnsucht. Sehnsucht. In August I waste an hour trying to find an elegant translation for the German word *Sehnsucht*, which means, basically, an inconsolable yearning for happiness and the unattainable.

I pass a Wetherspoons with a massive queue for Eat Out to Help Out. Dishy Rishi's Sunak Specials. You don't have to be an oracle to see how that one will pan out.

Jason keeps going out for beers and complains about having to download a different app every time and give all his details. He goes out with Toby, who works for a City bank for fuck's sake, and Toby's phone runs out of battery so Jason has to buy all the rounds. Toby and Meesha have got back together and come over for dinner, which is briefly allowed, with a bottle of expensive Lebanese red. Jason looks handsome that evening – I can't tell whether it's because he's wearing a shirt or talking to someone other than me.

Unsurprisingly, when the A-level results come out, academic clearing becomes absolute chaos, and my university doesn't know what to do. Thousands of weeping state-school children who were predicted Bs get Ds and so fail to get places in their chosen universities. It turns out they have decided on the grades using an algorithm, $Pkj = (1 - rj)Ckj + rj(Ckj + qkj - pkj)$. In this, Ckj is the historical grade distribution at the school over the last three years, 2017–19. So pupils are having their grades based on how people at their school have done previously. The trouble is that previous pupils might have had bad exam days, but none of these pupils *had* bad exam days. There was no exam day. It's the government saying to thousands of working-class kids: you might have been predicted an A, but you seem to us like the kind of person who is likely to fuck up their life chances, so we'll just assume you did.

Prediction by data is humanity's most accurate prophetic system, but it can't cope with individuals. It doesn't work with individuals.

Of course, this is just the start, I rant in various contexts. Soon our whole lives will be circumscribed by the prophecies of data: our jobs, housing, travel, freedoms. The pandemic is the excuse every government needs to track us, our every move and interaction. In China AI can scan the street for temperatures now; recognize faces even with masks. *One resident complained on Weibo his code had inexplicably changed from green to yellow, indicating he must quarantine. 'I can't even go out to get bread or water.'* In Sichuan a mah-jong party is forced to read an apology on video: 'We were wrong. We promise not to do it again and we will also monitor others.' In the Xinjiang region I read there is 'predictive policing'. A database that includes information such as people's personal preference for using the front or back door. You can be flagged for receiving a four-minute phone call from your sister abroad or being 'born after the 1980s'.

It is the summer of Black Lives Matter. Black Instagram squares. Trump calls BLM a 'symbol of hate' and calls in the National Guard. A memo goes round the Classics department that we need more students of colour, but no one applies through clearing. I guess why would they, I mean – our definition of 'Classics' is pretty abhorrent. It's mainly the usual private-school kids, all of whom seem to have improved on their predicted grades. Even on the phone I can hear their air of ski lifts and private pools; their costly, unremarkable clothes. They drop *Audentes fortuna iuvat* into our interviews like they're fucking Boris Johnson.

Gastromancy:
Prophecy by Guttural Sounds

Representation of Women in Classical Mythology is always a very popular course, and I have to put together a lecture on Medea and then try to film it without hating my own piggy eyes with those ridiculous shadows and the thick white streak in my home-trimmed fringe. I forget to close a wardrobe door properly in the backdrop. Drilling starts. I actually burp in one take and have to start again.

Medea. Barbarian, from the Greek *barbaroi*: 'babbler', an onomatopoeic word for foreigners whose words sound like 'bar-bar'. The ultimate outsider. In mythology, she is always depicted as some kind of sorceress. Descendant of the sun god Helios, relation of the witch Circe. She helps Jason to win the golden fleece, abandoning (murdering?) her own family in the process, marries him and has sons by him, only for him to leave her for a good Greek princess – Glauce, the daughter of Creon, the king. In her rage, the tale has it, she kills Glauce with a poisoned gift, then slaughters her own children.

Gathering the evidence for and against her, I put together extracts from various texts. The playwright Euripides, of course – a couple of speeches, including the bit where she claims: 'I'd three times sooner go to war than suffer childbirth once.' Then the Latin interpretations. Medea's letter to Jason from Ovid's *Heroides*, in the poet Clare Pollard's translation:

> It seems I can tame serpents
> but not a man.
> I held back fire with my enchantments
> but cannot stand the melt of my own lust.

Seneca's Medea saying, 'Though I slay two, it's not enough to satisfy this grief. If in my womb there is still evidence of you, I'll search my very insides with this sword and haul it forth.' (An influence on Lady Macbeth there, surely.)

Medea's filicide revolts us because it is impossible. Because we sympathize and then we feel tricked. We can't believe she kills her children deliberately; it goes against our every instinct. How can she look in their faces and do it?

But she didn't, of course. There is no Medea. Or, she wasn't like Medea. There are men like her, men who kill their children deliberately in an act of vengeance against their wives leaving them – who strap the children in the car and drive off a cliff. But not women. Crazed women maybe, like Agave tearing off Pentheus' head, god-maddened into thinking him a mountain lion, or poor Gretchen in Goethe's *Faust*, drowning her bastard baby in delusion. Women suffering psychosis. But not sane women, on purpose. Medea is not an archetype. She is Euripides' singular monster.

In earlier accounts, Medea killed her children by accident, perhaps when hiding them from Jason. That's a horror that rings true. Many women kill their children by accident, don't they? I sometimes wonder if I'll be one of them. Not checking some ingredient list closely enough. Trusting some server at Pret.

More traditionally, they were killed by the Corinthians after her escape, stoned to death in vengeance for Glauce's murder. Doesn't that sound more likely too? But once fake news is out there you can't put it back. *Lock her up! Lock her up!*

Or some say that Zeus fell in love with Medea, but she spurned his advances. Hera, in gratitude, said: 'I will make your children immortal if you lay them on the sacrificial altar of my temple.' Just a little scratch of death, then; a bargain like a vaccination. Their souls became immortal.

In the first century BC, a historian called Diodorus Siculus wrote that, 'Speaking generally, it is because of the desire of the tragic poets for the marvellous that so varied and inconsistent an account of Medea has been given out.' But maybe even that is a generous excuse. Legend has it that Euripides put the blame on to Medea because Corinthians bribed him with a payment of five talents.

Shufflemancy: Prophecy by the Use of an Electronic Media Player

I'm entering a Tesco when I see an anti-mask protest. QUESTION THE NARRATIVE. LOCKDOWN KILLS. CURFEWS EQUAL NAZIFICATION. I think I'm supposed to consider them alt-right villains, screaming their virus in everyone's faces, but I feel a twinge of sympathy at their hand-painted signs. I just put my head down, keep listening to Spotify. We laugh at conspiracy theorists, but aren't there powers conspiring against us? I feel that there are. I feel that chill of powerlessness as the machine of this world cranks and chews.

Do not remove card.

Please remove card.

Where they're probably wrong is in this insistence on a small elite directing the action. But there have always been such fantasies – Madame Blavatsky, for example, the famous nineteenth-century occultist who founded Theosophy, taught that there is an ancient, secret brotherhood of spiritual adepts known as the Masters, found across the world but centred in Tibet. Hilma af Klint, one of my favourite artists, was interested in Blavatsky's ideas. I have her *Altarpiece No. 1, Group X* on my pinboard in my shared office at university. Af Klint was part of a circle of women called 'The Five' who received messages from spirits called the High Masters. She believed that her best work – her radiant, holy abstractions – were directed by a force that would literally guide her hand. The High Masters making art for their temple.

We all hallucinate that there is someone in charge, a good master or a bad, it doesn't matter, as long as they understand the plan. We just want these fragments to cohere. Af Klint's *Altarpiece* is so beautiful in its simplicity, far too beautiful to be true.

Spotify plays Lizzo's 'Juice' when I pick up some juice, which I guess is a coincidence.

Cleromancy:
Prophecy by Random Numbers

The hollyhocks are very tall, their swords waving above my head. Bees putter around the garden as I hang up the washing: towels, T-shirts, PlayStation underpants. It's idyllic in a way, I know. I'm not supposed to say anything this year without immediately prefacing it with 'I realize how lucky we are to have a garden'.

On my lunch break after trying to persuade Xander to eat his bacon and toast in the sunlight, I decide to tug some weeds out of the front garden, and go round there with my bucket and shovel only to find my I Ching package flung into a lavender bush at the side, the box very, very soggy from last night's rainstorm. I'd thought it had gone missing; had been about to reorder it.

Once the box has dried out, I take it upstairs, then sit in our bedroom and shut the door like I am masturbating.

The I Ching or The Book of Changes began as a divination manual in the period of the Chou dynasty (1040–223 BC). The Chou rulers proclaimed they had a 'Mandate of Heaven'. The text changed over the years that followed with the addition of philosophical commentaries known as 'The Ten Wings'. The most important part of this, the Great Commentary, associates knowledge of the I Ching with the ability to 'delight in Heaven and understand fate'. I have read that the numbers were drawn using yarrow stalks at first, although we don't know how the stalks became numbers. Now people sometimes use coins or dice. Six numbers between 6 and 9 are turned into a hexagram.

I read in the introduction that we are descended from dragons. The hexagrams are dragon-language. Dragon-graphs. The solid lines are male (*yang*) and the divided ones female (*yin*). The hexagrams reveal the interactions of heaven and earth; they let us 'place ourselves' within change. The I Ching shows us we are each a fleeting shape within the perpetual churn of transformation.

The yarrow sticks are less impressive. I wish I'd read the reviews before I clicked buy. They cost twelve pounds or something and are just a bunch of twigs kept together with an elastic band. *These are indeed sticks,* reads the first review. *If they looked just like the sticks in the picture they would not be worth 12 pounds, but I wouldn't be leaving this poor review. However my sticks are of differing diameter, splintered with uneven edges. They are sloppily whittled.*

I manage to work out how to make a hexagram, though, with the help of wikiHow, and then check it in the book.

It is 28, Excessive Pressure. 'Under excessive pressure, the roof begins to sag.' I can't say this feels much like a revelation. I just think: well, yes, it does.

A few days later, I find an app. You can just press a button six times, and each time it throws three 'coins', and then it spits out a hexagram and a little fortune. The trouble is, it's too easy if you don't like the fortune to just do it again and again. I feel like an addict in an arcade, pushing in coin after coin, waiting for those cherries to line up. Like I'm chomping fortune cookie after cookie to get to words I want.

What words do I want anyway? What do we want, all of us, pressing these buttons, scrolling for our fates? Which words would sate us? *Things will get better. You will be happier. Love is coming. It will be okay.*

Ceneromancy: Prophecy by the Ashes of a Specifically Ritual Fire

Though I tell myself the clairvoyance thing is just a hobby, or a writing exercise, I still keep it my shameful secret. Men don't like a sorceress, do they? Least of all Jason, Jesus. I mean, he's actually called *Jason*! Also, is doing the I Ching a bit racist, in a cultural appropriation way?

Some days I tell myself it's fun, though it could suddenly not be. As a teenager I loved the Confessional poet Sylvia Plath, who we studied at A level. I loved her tarot poem, 'The Hanging Man'. I loved the idea of her and her husband – Ted Hughes, also a poet – doing the Ouija board; receiving messages from her spirit guide, Pan, who predicted her next book would be published by Knopf. Plath's whole life, in fact, seemed delicious to me back then – how they moved to the countryside, had amazing sex (it was implied), made babies, ate rabbit, harvested daffodils, whilst always dabbling with the occult, using it in their brutally good poems. They had their astrological charts made; Ted hypnotized her before childbirth.

The critic Al Alvarez claims that, in the last days before her suicide, the black magic took Plath over. When Ted had an affair with Assia Wevill, Plath took his manuscripts, mixed them with fingernail cuttings and dandruff from his desk, then burned them in a ritual bonfire, only for a fragment of paper to drift to her with a single word: *Assia*.

It was a vicious winter and she must have felt very isolated in her flat. Her two small children were asleep when she wedged wet towels around the kitchen door and put her head in the oven. There is something about the scene's domestic detail that haunts me: that German word, *unheimlich* – often translated as 'uncanny', but also meaning 'unhomely'. Home gone wrong . . .

Whatever, I've hardly got Plath's soul inside me, have I? I'm not a poet. I'm not going to become some supernatural addict – *I'm too boring for that*, I sneer at myself. Still, I somehow know it's important not to make a ritual; not to take things seriously. Not to acknowledge those hovering weapons. I mean, I don't *actually* think I'm a prophetess LOL. I'm supposed to use some special pouch, but I stuff the shitty yarrow sticks in my bottom drawer next to my vibrator.

Nephomancy: Prophecy by Clouds

Strange geek girl, doodling dragons, nose in an Ursula Le Guin. *Head in the clouds*. Growing up, I recall cherishing the idea that I would discover the meaning of life. Are all children like that, certain of some special destiny, or was I particularly arrogant? Perhaps the latter. Dark lank hair tucked behind my ears.

A couple of times I really thought I'd got it, I mean, *really*. Because it's so strange, isn't it, that out of all of history and all of the billions who have lived on this planet, I am me, now – but then I realized 'I' always exist, 'I' am always looking out of my eyes, and as long as a person exists in the world I will exist and will be looking out and wondering at the fluke of my existing in this body looking through these eyes.

No, I've not articulated it right. I can't quite. It always looks stupid once I write it. It's more a feeling than something you can put into words, a feeling that rises then subsides. Once I tried to explain it to the girl who sat next to me at school, which didn't go that well. I've not tried to explain it again since.

It's funny how Jason has absolutely no idea what's going on in my head.

I mean, not that funny, and I don't know what's in his either, but we spend so long together in this same space and he doesn't even know when I'm thinking about Andromache or whatever. We don't talk about my work at all. He used to enjoy me serving him up the odd juicy little fact at least, but now I'll start to tell Jason that Homer's blindness might be the reason he seems unaware of the colour blue in his poems and his eyes glaze, like when my mother's telling him a long anecdote about the daughter of someone at her church. I'll be thinking about some aspect of Stoicism and he just shouts out a question about the shopping list: *Did you write down Shreddies?*

When I first had Xander, that was when I started to notice this mismatch between what was going on in my head and how the world saw me. I'd be at soft play and some random attendant would say, 'Cheer up, Mum,' or something, and it was like: *Can't they see I'm meditating on the death of Socrates?* Ha! Which, obviously, fully makes me sound like a stuck-up twat. Now I'm in my mid-forties I don't suppose most people wonder what's in my head at all, or if they do they just think it's calories and flavoured gin.

I finished the German translation a day ago, a summer's work: pressed send. Now it's that unpleasant couple of weeks whilst I wait for the publisher and author's representatives to read it and respond, both wanting them to and not wanting them to. At the end the Faust character didn't descend into the fires of hell, he accepted a job at Google.

'I'll just be relieved when Xander starts school again,' Jason says, opening some can of craft beer then slurping the foam off the rim. Elvis Juice. Tiny Rebel. Some sad little name. 'I've been worried about him.'

'Have you?' I say, picking up an onion from the vegetable rack. I begin to chop it for the usual pasta.

The sky through the kitchen window is apricot with small violet clouds.

'What does that mean?' Jason asks. 'Of course I have, he needs his friends, he clearly isn't very happy. It's too much screen time for him, he keeps getting tearful.'

'He's reading every day, he's doing his maths, I make him exercise, we play board games. Xander cooked burgers with me last week, it's not my fault if he –'

'I wasn't blaming you, it isn't about you,' his voice says behind me, running the tap to wash up.

'What's that supposed to mean?' I demand. Doesn't he even see? The guilt I feel, the hours I put in. 'Maybe it *is* about me. Maybe it's about me doing all the fucking home-schooling, all his teas, ferrying him to all his play dates over summer, trying to take him to the park and to fucking Go Ape and clubs and everything because you have to work, even though I have to work too, but apparently no one in this house gives a shit about that.'

'Of course I do. Do you think I want to be in these utterly boring Zoom meetings? They're draining the life out of me. I'm trying to keep my job.'

'Whereas my job, which pays virtually the same, I'm just supposed to fit it in scraps of time like a hobby?'

'No! Do your job. Let him play games like I do. That's what everyone else does, that's what he wants to do. Stop being a fucking martyr. It doesn't help, does it? Our son's still depressed.'

'It does fucking help, actually,' I spit. 'It would be a fuck of a lot worse if I hadn't done all that stuff. It does fucking help a lot, it's you who doesn't help.'

'That's what I – ugh. Yeah, whatever. Don't listen to a word I say, you never do.'

A clatter of forks. The tap stops. I hear him leave the room, slurping his beer again. I realize I never even looked at his face, though I saw the shape of him on the glass, against the blotchy sunset sky.

Aeromancy: Prophecy by Air

Aristotle's *Poetics* tells us that in tragedy the tragic hero always has a hamartia – a tragic flaw; a mistake. It comes from the Greek term *hamartanein*, for an archer missing his target. At the end the tragic hero has a moment of anagnorisis. A change from ignorance to awareness. They realize what they have done.

One week, I make the mistake of reading *The Uninhabitable Earth* by David Wallace-Wells because it's a cheap download on Kindle. It is a book of prophecy based on the parts per million (ppm) of atmospheric carbon dioxide. I learn that Jakarta, home to 10 million, could be entirely underwater by 2050. Every return flight from London to New York will cost the Arctic three square metres of ice. I read: heat death; dying oceans; unbreathable air; plagues; burning forests; psychological trauma; societal collapse. A great migration. A great dying.

But the thing is, there are levels. Limbo < Suffering < Purgatory < Abyss < Hell < Inferno. If we stop now we can end in some lesser circle, stop ourselves from entering the centre of horror.

Every page I turn I think of anagnorisis. Most of the damage has been done in my lifetime. Briefly, I see what I have done. I have done it to the next generation; to Xander, my own child. But then I go to the supermarket and no other adult appears to have seen. Every person looks ignorant; every person fills their trolley with plastic-wrapped meat and tat and imports, doubling down on their harmartia. My vision dissipates, I can feel it drain away.

At the beginning of the pandemic people thought it might help. They could see the stars in Delhi, remember that? Emissions fell by seventeen per cent at the peak of lockdown. But now the streets teem with cars and delivery vans; China's manufacturing is back to strength. *The lockdown-related fall in emissions is just a tiny blip on the long-term graph.* We have squandered our anagnorisis. We have returned it with our pre-paid shipping label.

Cyclicomancy: Prophecy by Swirling Water in a Cup

In bed by nine with a cup of weak herbal tea, bored, whilst Jason watches TV downstairs and probably gets the vodka out or has a sneaky joint or something like I'm his fucking headmistress.

I decide to take a red pill and a blue pill.

It takes me a while to get to sleep. My back hurts at the moment, I feel clammy. Foxes. But then I must fall asleep because I dream I am in Delphi, beneath those shining rocks. A dry riverbed, olive trees that rustle, a scent of thyme.

Led towards the fissure by men, I realize it is me: I am the oracle; the ordinary middle-aged woman they have chosen as oracle. As we enter the cave I stoop as if bowing to something, my eyes trying to focus in the darkness, my sandals cautious on the uneven stone floor. And then there is a rising, gagging feeling – something trickling into my belly at first, then in my blood, my lungs. 'Ugggghhh,' I blurt, breathing quicker, vision skittering. 'Urrrr . . .'

Apollo speaks through me in a surge: I feel him clack my jaw and writhe my tongue in my mouth as Ancient Greek words pour pour pour

He says / I say: the second wave comes, more monstrous than the first

He says / I say: a leader will lose but refuse to leave

He says / I say, through my lips: clouds of sulphuric acid 55 degrees Celsius

He says/ I say: people lying baked by the road their insides cooked . . . the smell . . . water queues where a credit is a small plastic bottle of yellowish water . . . mothers with babies wait with stagnant eyes . . . only the wealthy will have taps in their grand hilltop houses . . .

And as I puke out these words I am remembering Xander in literally inches of bubbly water, kicking, sucking flannel, *if you're happy and you know it splash your hands*, lit water pouring pouring from stacky cup to stacky cup and raining down his neck or the apricots from Cape Town I washed for Xander under taps.

Apollo does not have anything to say about my marriage. It is as meaningless to the gods as this grain of white dust; this olive stone spat into sand.

Necromancy:
Prophecy by Speaking to the Dead

'Ouija' is a trademark of Hasbro. The Ouija board was considered an innocent parlour game before a spiritualist called Pearl Curran began to commune with the dead through it in 1913. I own one, but the planchette is sticky and unresponsive. I always wonder, when I bring it out at Halloween, if the spirits are my responsibility. *Am I failing to grasp that as hostess I have to improvise a quick message from the dead?*

There are very detailed instructions in the British Library. To communicate with the dead you must first take a skull.

Crush mouldy wood and leaves of the Euphrates poplar in water, beer and oil. Add crushed and sieved snake tallow, lion tallow, crab tallow, white honey, a frog, a hair of dog, a cat and a fox, bristle of chameleon, bristle of red lizard, left wing of a grasshopper, marrow from the long bone of a goose. Smear this ointment on your eyes. Repeat three times: 'O skull of skulls: May he who is within the skull answer me.'

It sounds too complicated to even attempt. But no harder than making anyone come to life, I suppose. Think of the months of stealthy care that go into conjuring a baby: the right sperm, a good egg, a healthy womb, folic acid, vitamin D, no lifting, no liver and bacon, a midwife-led unit, gas and air, a TENS machine, agony beyond words, skin to skin, an umbilical clamp, ergometrine jabbed in your thigh to safely remove the placenta. Heat it in a glass coffin. Wean exclusively on human colostrum, hand expressed drop by drop into a cup.

I think I made a misstep in the spell the second time. A little coffee, bagged salad, a medium-rare steak. Perhaps it was that glass of wine. Some wrong ingredient. I remember having a glass of wine and thinking perhaps this will kill my baby, but then thinking that fear was a kind of protection. Like, the glass of wine couldn't kill my baby, because that would be too much of a coincidence. Or maybe I almost thought it was win–win. Like if the baby died, at least that would be proof of supernatural powers, which might be a comfort. But the thing I feared just happened anyway, and the comfort prescience offers turns out to be very limited.

My daughter had a skull, little red.

*

In my garden there is an autumn cherry tree. I bought one because I thought the idea romantic. Blossom in October, like a metaphor for hope. But now I see blossom mixed up with the autumn leaves and I want to cry with pity. It's not fair to be blossoming just as the world darkens and rots, for new life to be so mixed in with death.

Xander is back at school but he's not really enjoying it, he says it's 'boringer' than before. They work at separate desks; they can't take bags in. Every day at three I have to walk over and stand in the yard by the front gate with my mask on. All the parents standing two metres from each other, scrolling through their phones. Having to take a glove off to use the phone and tap in their security code because the facial recognition doesn't work. When the children come out they line up in the playground and a male teacher sends them to their adult one at a time, I suppose having recognized whose parents are there, although I don't know how he recognizes anyone – we all have our hoods up and the same disposable masks.

They give me a parent phone call, which is about fucking time, and they say they are worried about his mental health. I want to say, *You didn't seem worried for six whole months, you didn't even glance at his work to see how he was doing.*

A woman's voice in my kitchen, weary, old. One of his teachers, I guess, the names temporarily escape me. They job share, and we don't see them in person now there's this Covid-secure gate system. She says there's been a rise in self-harm amongst children during the pandemic, some even primary school age, so they're making sure parents are aware of the warning signs. Today Xander got very angry at himself. They told him off for messing around with the hand sanitizer, and he started clawing at himself; punching himself. He said he hated himself.

'He claws at himself a lot,' I tell them. 'It's his allergies. Did you give him his mittens? He has these mittens in his bag for when he's really bad. You do have his bag, right?'

'I wonder is he experiencing anxiety? What about his dreams?'

Right, I'm supposed to monitor his dreams now too! What about my own dreams? I want to rant: heaven forbid there might be a couple of hours in the night I don't feel the full weight of my responsibility for his mortal existence. I mean, what does she expect me to reply? Oh, I've got one, when he was six he woke up screaming because a sandwich was chasing him.

Googlemancy: Prophecy by Strangers

What will the new normal **look like uk**

Will the new normal **last forever**

Masks are the new normal

Visors and facial protection will be integrated into the uniforms of postal workers, delivery people, grocery store clerks, police, firefighters, and security guards

Queuing is the new normal

Outdoor waiting lines will be ubiquitous, in front of grocery and retail stores, museums, cultural venues, and especially office buildings, whose occupants will have to wait to have their temperatures checked

Hand sanitizer is the new normal

Elbow bumps are the new normal

Kissing non-sexually will no longer be normal

Blended learning is the new normal

Paying contactless is the new normal

Shopping online is the new normal

Virtual teamwork is the new normal

There will be substantial queues in office lobbies to avoid overcrowding in the elevator

Social distancing for a prolonged period means that the costs of restaurants, cinemas or plays will become high as a result of reduced seating. The rich will secure personal chefs and private concerts whilst the poor will be effectively shut out of such pleasures

Optimists hope that this collective nightmare will bring a renewed political focus on what makes life worth living

Higher taxes will be the new normal

Track and Trace will be the new normal

Will the new normal **be permanent**

Osteomancy: Prophecy by Bones

They make us go back in to teach for the first couple of weeks. It's so utterly ridiculous. We've proven we can deliver education online, but the thing is, the students pay hardly any of their money towards teaching. What they pay for is the big shiny buildings with the libraries and computer access and cafes and student-living accommodation, and if they don't get that, nine thousand pounds a year is suddenly going to look a lot for what it is: a few contact hours with harassed staff on underpaid, short-term contracts. They actually make the students come to the university, even though they know it's going to be a total shitshow.

Within two weeks Covid-19 has torn around the halls of residence. Flats have notes stuck up in their windows saying WE HAVE CORONA and SEND ALCOHOL, like plague marks on doors during the Black Death. I hear complaints the self-isolating kids are being charged £18 for daily food boxes worth under a fiver: a plastic-wrapped croissant, a tiny carton of juice with a straw, an energy bar, a sandwich, a pot noodle. The cleaners are always deep-cleaning, always on their knees. Empty corridors; white noise of vacuum cleaners; a bottle of disinfectant and a little cloth by every fire door. I have seminars where only two of the ten students come in, and the window only opens an inch for ventilation and I'm wearing this stupid face shield.

Afterwards I have to check the online breakout rooms, and type that calling Medea a 'feminist' is perhaps a misreading.

*

I'm trying to limit the I Ching to once a day. I go to the app and press six times every morning.

And then click through possible interpretations. This is 30, Separation. Or no, Radiance. Or no, something or someone clinging like fire. Which interpretation do I pick? Which do I choose to discard and forget?

Maybe it would be more useful to my actual research if I was using Greek methods of divination every day. I mean, if this is seriously research I should get myself some sheep's knuckles.

*

It turns out that our world-beating 12-billion-pound Test and Trace system is being run on Excel. Excel! This comes to light when people who test positive aren't recorded, after a master Excel spreadsheet reaches its maximum size of 16,384 columns.

It's hard not to pour a glass of something strong at six or how is the evening distinct from the daytime? Once Xander's in his room, reading, I start putting together a seminar on Cassandra with a glass of white. Jason is meeting friends for a beer in some beer garden or other. He comes back coked up although he says he isn't. Still all hyped with anger at everyone and with a bag of fried chicken from Morley's.

Heading up to bed to leave him with his chicken bones, I masturbate with the vibrator, thinking of Tiresias, touching her slick cunt as her cock thrusts into me over and over, breasts in my mouth, the wet violet head of the shaft blooming, waves of wet, man-woman, woman-man.

Ophiomancy: Prophecy by Snake

Poor Cassandra. The prophetess who no one listens to or believes.

My Twitter is full of Cassandras now. The more they tweet *The Worst-Case Scenario for Global Warming Tracks Closely with Actual Emissions* the less traction their tweets get. The more they look like misinformation. Or maybe they're enjoying the disaster too much, right? And me too, when I hear myself saying: 'test and trace is permanent, they're creating a surveillance state where you'll need to scan a QR code to visit your sister' or I RT *Deforestation in Brazil's Amazon rainforest has skyrocketed to a 12-year high in 2020* – in these moments I feel that I am both Cassandra and the person who absolutely won't or can't believe her.

Melanie Klein, the psychologist, introduced the idea that Cassandra represents the human conscience, pointing out moral infringements and their consequences. For her, the metaphor applies to those predictions which provoke in others 'a refusal to believe what they know to be true, expressing the universal tendency to denial as a potent defence against persecutory guilt and anxiety'.

Cassandra, daughter of Troy. Sister of Hector the hero. In one origin story she gains her powers when a snake licks her ears. In another, Apollo gives her the power to see the future as an enticement to sex. But as Hyginus writes in his *Fabulae*: 'Cassandra is said to have fallen asleep when Apollo wished to embrace her, so did not afford the opportunity of her body.' Unable to fuck her, Apollo curses her instead. She will always be disbelieved, as women are in such situations.

At the fall of Troy, she is raped in the Temple of Athena by Ajax the Lesser. Great name, Ajax! Even Athena cannot restrain her tears and her roar shakes the floor of the temple. Her statue averts its eyes.

Next Cassandra becomes a concubine to King Agamemnon, whose wife at last, despite Cassandra's repeated warnings, kills her. To always know what will be done to you, but never be believed. #Believewomen right? (Must work that into my seminar, interest gen Z . . .)

The German novelist Christa Wolf wrote a stunning novel, *Cassandra*. Cassandra discovers that Helen is not in Troy, and the premise for the whole war is a lie. Her Troy is a police state like the one Wolf grew up with in East Germany, in which Cassandra is powerless to oppose the political forces that spread propaganda.

> In the middle of a war you think of nothing but how it will end. And put off living [. . .] What I regret more

than anything else is that, in the beginning, I too gave in to the feeling that for now I was living only provisionally; that true reality still lay ahead of me: I let life pass me by.

(Trans. Jan van Heurck)

I type this quote into my seminar resources and feel the tears smarting in my eyes. For myself. For us.

Tasseography: Prophecy by Tea Leaves or Coffee Grounds

Once, I thought Xander would die. I stumbled into A&E like Mary in the pietà, cradling his body, its tiny wheezing swollen mouth and fat tongue. When they saw his oxygen levels, within seconds there were suddenly twenty medics jostling around us with equipment, talking rapidly, carrying out a series of urgent tests.

Things had stabilized later, after midnight, when I was given a fold-out bed next to his in the children's ward. But still, listening to the rapid bleep of the monitor, I don't think I've ever been so awake: all those garish cartoon characters grinning on the shadowy walls; those adults trying to keep fear out of their whispers; the snotty screams. It was hell. The thought kept repeating in my head: *I am in hell.* The coffee from the machine tasted exactly like you'd expect the coffee in hell to taste. Afterwards I was a mess for a long time. I thought Xander would die many many times. He was so beautiful and vulnerable it was intolerable.

I'm making my morning pot of coffee when I catch him watching a video on YouTube. God knows how many hours he's been up already, staring. A weeping Minion is slitting his wrists, blood spurting everywhere. Xander's laughing at it over a slice of toast. I crash across the kitchen and switch it off, shaking. 'For God's sake, Xander, I told you no screens before school, how did you even find that crap?' I shouldn't swear. When he was four he kept calling junk 'crup' at his nursery.

'I just clicked on it, it's kind of funny,' he says. His hair is almost at his shoulders, I have to snip it before he gets nits again: buy some hairdressing scissors, think up some bribe. I realize it's probably one of those uncanny videos made by algorithms that have been scaring parents, where Peppa Pig drinks bleach or eats her father. Paw Patrol pups get decapitated.

'Well don't just click on any old stuff,' I say. 'There's evil people out there. That channel's full of lies and filth.'

'Mum, you downloaded the app for me when I was three. Anyway, it's a Minion! Minions are meant to be evil. That's what makes them cute!'

'It's not a Minion, it just looks like a Minion, but it's a fake Minion,' I say, and then he grins, and I listen to myself and can't stay angry. His long lashes. It sounds so cheesy but sometimes him smiling is the only genuinely nice thing that happens to me all day, though lately it's a rare treat.

*

We need a circuit-break lockdown NOW people tweet into the ether. Not me, though, I just let the words slide past me.

I'm so bored of being in my head, or of gazing at books or screens, which is being in someone else's head. Nothing feels at all real. I think of the philosopher Hannah Arendt: 'Action, as distinguished from fabrication, is never possible in isolation; to be isolated is to be deprived of the capacity to act.' All this fabrication. We're all in Plato's cave, chained to the blank wall, staring endlessly at the shadows.

Zoom drinks have petered out, the quizzes and parties, now it's just the identical autumn nights of wine and TV and Jason making me rewatch *The Wire*. Well, that or I watch virtual tours of secondary schools for Xander's online application, as if we actually have a choice and places aren't decided by the distance calculator on Google Maps. The videos all use the same plinky copyright-free music and sped-up footage. I hurtle dutifully down identical institutional corridors; through double door after double door.

I keep saying I'm going to volunteer at a food bank or something but I don't. I have lower back ache from sitting all day, and try yoga videos on YouTube with Adriene, who I notice uses the word 'yummy' a lot: downward dog, warrior one, child's pose. Every morning I throw the coffee grounds from my cafetière on the garden, even though I don't know if it's a good thing that will keep away cats and slugs, or if it will actually turn my soil acid. I don't know why I don't google it. Sometimes I look inside the pot, trying to find a form in there.

Tasseography. From the French *tasse* for 'cup'.

I've given up on the I Ching for now, anyway, but I pick up the tarot pack again, having impulse-ordered a book called *Tarot Today* by Colette Lee. I'm nervous, somehow, to lay a spread for myself. I'm still remembering that last card I drew, the Ten of Cups: *contentment, repose of the entire heart; the perfection of that state*, and it's as though I don't want to jinx it; to supersede it. To turn it from what will be to what was. But I remember that Nine of Swords too, that Nine of Swords I've been studiously ignoring or dismissing, what if I get it again and that means it's true?

Colette seems very nice, a bit cheesy. At first I'm a bit put off by some of the advice – get thee a big pink crystal, bake cookies with poppy seeds for compassion – it's all slightly fey self-care, but then I read what she says about Tens – how they are about a cycle ending and always tinged with boredom and that sense of 'what next?' and I get that little thrill of it being true, which I guess is what I'm always hunting.

Sat on my bed, on the teal duvet cover, rain on the roof, I make myself pull a card:

Strength. A woman petting a lion.

I check the book. Colette says it represents our inner wildness, and means I'm probably struggling with it. I must bring my wildness under control.

But isn't that what I've done all year, what we've all done, with this self-imposed imprisonment, obedient little children waiting for Daddy to tell us we're allowed a haircut or a play date?

There are lots of tarot people on Twitter. Late one night, whilst semi-watching *Have I Got News For You*, I find myself reading about tarot apps and cut and paste it in my notes:

Courtney Quint, coder of Cunning Tarot, uses a random algorithm for choosing the cards in her app, which she illustrated herself. When a user draws their cards, they are prompted to input emotional state and other reflections, with the app tracking this information over time to give insight into mental wellbeing as a menstrual app might. Their user-responsive code also bases readings on behaviour such as screen taps—and a magic spell Courtney had embedded into a junk code by a Wiccan priest!

*

The world, though. The world. It's still there, apparently, with real things happening in it. In California the forests are blazing; firefighters critically injured. Priti Patel keeps appearing to stab some new poppet with a pin.

Then Trump has Covid. *Tonight, @FLOTUS and I tested positive for COVID-19. We will begin our quarantine and recovery process immediately. We will get through this TOGETHER!* Twitter is abuzz. He's flown to the Walter Reed Military Medical Center and everyone is tweeting that it's either a hoax or he's going to die. Ivanka and Eric put out a statement, he's a 'Warrior'. He's taken oxygen twice. He's on dexamethasone.

I purposefully use my MAKE ROME GREAT AGAIN mug for my morning coffee, swirling the grounds.

The Roman Emperor Nero did not, as people often say, fiddle whilst Rome burned – the fiddle was not invented until 1,400 years later. Instead, the rumour was that he sang 'Sack of Illium' in full stage costume. Suetonius writes that Nero started the fire himself, because he wanted the space to build his Golden House.

Everyone is watching America. Trump is every headline. Trump is every update. Washington is Delphi, and we wait to hear our future. They call it Omphalos Syndrome: the belief that a place of geopolitical power is the most important place in the world.

I know he's not going to die, though. Apollo says / I say: a leader will lose but refuse to leave. How can I save the world from him? On Sunday, Trump makes a surprise appearance in a drive-past, waving at supporters outside the hospital.

Astrology:
Prophecy by Celestial Bodies

We are obeying the rule of six when Jay and I have a drink after work at their hotel across the road from the university, after a departmental meeting. They used to commute in from Essex for their two days a week contact hours, but all the trains back and forth are giving them anxiety attacks so they're staying over on Wednesdays. 'They actually announced on the train today,' Jay says, 'we are in a metal tube, if someone sneezes at one end, someone at the other end could get Covid. Is that even true? They sounded like they were in a mortal panic.'

It's a couple of days before Tier 2. The hotel is corporate, big windows full of grey light; low-hanging lightshades; shiny coffee tables that look empty now they can't hand out complimentary bowls of nuts and olives. We sit on an aubergine sofa. Jay's sad because their girlfriend has been stuck in France all year; they managed to meet in Paris for a fortnight in the summer, that's it. I have that Negroni I've been wanting. The strong adult taste is delicious but the ice cubes get in my face. Jay goes for a bottle of beer, complimenting me on my Athena necklace as they sip. They were thirty in the summer. 'My Saturn return,' they say. 'Guess I need to work out what I'm doing with my life.'

'Yeah, all the forty-year-olds have it sorted,' I say, smiling.

Jay's girlfriend is Cancer, which means she does a lot of late-night texting and is into nipple clamps. Jay is a Leo, they're not a good sun-sign match.

I tell them, ish, about my prophecy project, though I don't mention the lucid dreams. I ask them lots of questions about astrology. I've been reading about how astrologers are the technicians of prophecy. It is a pseudo-science. Pseudo-empirical. They don't go into a wild trance, they make extremely complex and tedious mathematical charts. It's one of the modes of premonition that interests me least, all those spreadsheets. All those thrilling encounters that approximately five and a half million Aquarians in this country are somehow supposed to experience on the same wet Thursday. Even in Roman times, people were critical. Cicero argued that since the other planets are far more distant from the earth than the moon, surely the moon would have much more influence? He also argued that astrology ignores inherited ability, parenting, or the influence of physical factors such as health or weather on people's lives. I think they call it intersectionality now.

'Oh, I'm not sure I a hundred per cent believe it,' Jay says. 'I just find it a useful way to think about my life, you know?' We have another drink and then the bar says it has to shut, Covid compliance.

Jay has some cannabis and beer in their room. In the lift we are talking animatedly about the pitfalls of recording lectures; about our intellectual property. The mattress on their bed is soft and springy. The bed has white sheets and a tall, aubergine bedhead. There is a little window that looks out on the car park that we smoke through, blowing pale air into the grey light. I was expecting a joint, but it's CBD oil in one of those vape things. They touch against me as we lean out.

I don't know how it escalates after that; I can't remember the choreography, exactly, how I realize that they are seducing me. And then I think J. The letter. The prophecy. And it's like a permission slip has materialized in my hand. A coin on my tongue. Another drink, another vape

]
]
kissing vapour from their mouth
                    fulfil O Aphrodite
] then fingers rubbing burying slipping
                    child of Zeus, I beg you
beckoning in muscle
in dark pink juddering [
]
]

                    mad heart loose me from this pang
and J [
]
and no and please please now gods this [   ] [] []
[   ] [] [   ] [   ]

*

It is always afterwards, though. The present moment is so brief, sometimes it hardly seems worth it. It never seems to me to have real substance, like the past or future.

It is always afterwards and I am looking at the deep lines on my forehead in the strip-lit bathroom and washing my chin with soap; a hair on it. My pores look so large in this mirror.

Sex is so basic, the grinding meat of it, that it's unbelievable to me how people base their lives around this process. I always just feel kind of chastened afterwards. It might have been the best fuck I ever had but I feel grim, like I've eaten a big dirty burger.

Jay on the bed is an Olympian, glowy moon face and a white hotel robe. They are making green tea and taking their meds, popping a pill like a star on to their pink, pierced tongue, to make a new constellation. Already, they are texting their girlfriend, who they love, on their deft wrist a tattoo of the caduceus: the two serpents Tiresias found copulating entwined around a staff.

The word: copulating.

'I'm sorry,' I mumble, pulling my shirt on. 'That probably wasn't. I mean, thank you. It was great, you're beautiful. But I know you're with someone.' I feel awkward as fuck.

I want to get my ugliness out of this building and into the air.

'You too, right? You're married, right?' They tilt their head, kindly. They shrug. 'This year, though, this year.'

Anthropomancy:
Prophecy by Human Sacrifice

Calchas is the first known mantis or augur of Greek literature, appearing at the beginning of Book I of Homer's *Iliad*. He is employed by the Greek army; sifts through the guts of enemies after battle looking for intel. Calchas prophesizes that in order to gain a favourable wind for the Greek ships, Agamemnon must sacrifice his daughter, Iphigeneia, to appease Artemis.

Agamemnon calls him a 'prophet of evil' but he does it all the same. Lifts the knife over her navel. Slits his squirming daughter open on an altar. Her small moist teeth as she screams. Shrill hell; red spray. Who can fight destiny, amirite?

I scrabble together an abstract on Calchas and Cassandra for an online *Oresteia* conference, and then I dutifully stay up late putting it together without addressing any of the things I really want to talk about. Like: what must it have felt like on Agamemnon's face, that first stir of wind, when he closed his eyes?

Some say Calchas died of shame, or died of laughter.

Psephomancy:
Prophecy by Lots or Ballots

Zadie Smith, in her essays on the pandemic in *Intimations*, refers to this year as 'The Great Humbling'. The phrase sticks in my mind. I say it aloud whilst I'm boiling the kettle. I wonder who exactly has been humbled, though, because it doesn't seem to be Jeff Bezos.

Me, anyway, I feel humbled. I think about the lion on that tarot card: caging the lion; pulling the teeth out of the mangy old beast; putting the lion out of its misery.

There are news pieces about billions of Covid procurement deals passing through a 'high priority lane' which funnelled PPE contracts to Tory chums, but the corruption has been so explicit the whole time that any anger looks performative. My mum's put in Tier 3, though you can still eat out if it's a 'substantial meal'. London moves into Tier 2, which means no indoor mixing with other households. It lasts about a week and then they decide on a lockdown. The rules are changing so frequently now, the only argument the government seem to have left is Simon Says.

Hannah Arendt argues that, under totalitarianism, 'what people get used to is less the content of rules, a close examination of which would always lead them into perplexity, than the *possession* of rules under which to subsume particulars'. Because of this, inverted new values are taken on most easily by those who supported old ones – in Nazi Germany, 'thou shalt not kill' was reversed. Thou shalt work from home; thou shalt go back into your office before you bankrupt Pret.

I can't even, to be honest, comprehend the numbers any more: 300 deaths a day, 400, 500. In a country of 63 million people is that utterly horrifying or nothing at all? Perhaps it's both, it feels like both.

Learning at our university goes online. Restaurants shut again, pubs, cinemas, theatres. They're all complaining, rightly – they've spent so much money making themselves Covid-secure and now they are going to go bankrupt – but I can hardly register the pain of abstract businesses, at my desk in the kitchen still, microwaving my coffee for the third time, meeting after meeting, pleas for extensions, watching *The Queen's Gambit*. Duolingo email me a reminder to keep up my 250-day streak.

And the news just keeps coming, the endless news. News is our lives now. It gives our lives a narrative, in place of individual action – news has rushed in to fill the void. The US Election is upon us. Biden seems to be leading but the polls are very, very close, and there is nervousness that people might be lying about voting for Trump like they did last time, ashamed but not really of their secret racist hearts. Polls haven't had a very good record of accuracy recently; people are starting to realize they're a pseudo-science. Just another guessing game.

I worry how many secret hearts cheer at QAnon's great untruth: this crazed vision of Trump secretly battling a satanic 'Deep State' that will end with him leading abused children out of the non-existent cellar of a pizza restaur-ant like a reverse Pied Piper. Trump, who locks actual migrant children in actual cages.

Post arrives for me: spendy flowers and a Playmobil Athena. Jason has ordered a meal kit. It is my birthday, which means it's nearly Halloween already. This year, though, I don't need a Ouija board, I just touch my fingers gently to the Twitter timeline and see what it can say that makes the hairs on my neck stand up.

When the night of the election comes we stay up late late. I have bought in all the ingredients to make Negronis, which I drink straight up so I don't get any stupid ice up my nose. Apparently, if you switch up the gin for rye whisky it makes a boulevardier, which is more autumnal. I think I might make cocktails my lockdown hobby. I keep telling Jason that Trump will lose but refuse to leave. 'I know your theory,' he says. 'You've told me about ten times now.'

It's quite fun watching it with Jason for a bit – he cares more than I realized, I actually get to discuss politics without him looking bored. 'Rapist,' Jason says to the screen whenever Trump's face comes up, his tongue slightly heavy in his mouth. There is a cut on Jason's chin I don't ask about. He flags eventually when he realizes there aren't even going to be results until after two, going to bed before me for a change.

But there I am still, at four in the morning, the demon of history herself!

The demon of history watching the TV and flicking between the live feeds and Twitter on her phone, RTing *endorsed by the KKK, Putin and the Taliban*, always alert in case she misses something, some of this history pouring down the screens like rain or tears pour down, her fingers moving like she's killing a monster like this is a game she can win.

Pilimancy: Prophecy by the Patterns of Human Hairs

'If you count the legal votes, I easily win. If you count the illegal votes, they can try to steal the election from us.' He actually says that. He's trying to stage a coup, of course he is. My headache is so bad, coloured lights are twitching at the edges of my vision.

Xander keeps asking me to check if Biden's won yet. He hates Trump, I guess by osmosis, he shares memes about him: a photo that asks *Who wore it best?* and shows Trump and a hairy corncob. Xander is stalking the house, restless without play dates, but briefly happy when he kills a Hecatonchire in *Monster Quest*. I make him read a chapter of *Harry Potter*; point limply at the barely used skateboard by the door, with its graphic of eyeballs and slime.

Perhaps I'm getting the menopause early like I think my mother did. Or I'm perimenopausal at least, a lot of blood clots in the toilet; insomnia; distraction; flashes. There will be no second child. No more suckling tiny mouths. More hairs keep growing on my chin, thick like wires, and I pluck them out or sometimes even run a fucking razor over them. Each morning I scry in the mirror. I know what I see there now: no affairs, no flirtation, no more sex, no more love, no more milk, diminishment. The world and I diminishing together. Dying together. I masturbate once or twice thinking about Jay, but not really, it's hard to get hot and excited about something in the past. Something over.

Afterwards I go to Sainsbury's and then realize I've forgotten my mask and have to drive back home again. It's getting darker earlier and the air is wet. Lights rear and smash in the obsidian mirrors of puddles; smoked glass. London feels awash with cortisol.

Lampadomancy: Prophecy by Flame

Sweats in the night. I toss in the sheets, stinking of the body lotion I have basted my dried-out limbs in, drafting and redrafting a work email, making the edits that have been requested on the novel translation in my head.

Jason's snoring. Wind rattling something down the side passage. I take the red and blue pills at two in the morning, wash them down like sleeping pills against all instruction.

I redraft the email again – *my decision to use the second person in that passage was a deliberate decision to reflect* – then am somehow on the phone to my mother who says turn on the news. On the screen I see space rocket after space rocket thrusting off. A bright shuddering. 'They're leaving,' she says. 'They're leaving us.' And I'm trying to work out who they are but I can see them boarding, a pale elite: white skin, white suits. Subtle flashes of silver or gold. Astronauts, all of them leaving at once.

Then I drop the phone because I smell the smoke and need to shut the window. Outside, the crackle of orange flames. Smouldering grey ruins. Grass catching. The planet is burning burning, where is my son? I see it then. I know what this is. I know what this all is! I need to tell everyone.

I want to grab them by their T-shirts, plead, get them to see, but I run up and down the stairs looking for people and I'm all alone in the house, there's no one to tell.

I'm crying. I'm choking. Where is my son?

I need to tell him that Heaven and Hell are true.

They were always true, but they don't exist in space, they exist in time.

Anthroposcopy:
Prophecy by Physical Appearance

Like all dreams I recall, this dream disturbs me. I keep saying it over to myself the next day: *Heaven and Hell exist in time.* It seems like a profoundly true and yet useless piece of information, I don't know what to do with it.

I think my husband drank a bottle of vodka today. Well, maybe not a full bottle but maybe a full bottle. Also, I think he has a wrap of coke in the house, which – I mean it's not like we've never taken drugs before – but he's over forty and he's not telling me about it. His breath like a dragon's breath; a rotting body in a fissure.

Am I not concentrating? Am I in a trance?

Jason in the kitchen, his belly hanging over his pyjamas or are we calling it loungewear now.

That stale outside smell from smoking weed again. *Dirty woodburners*, Xander used to call them, snitching up his nose. Jason gave up for him when he was a toddler and he wanted to be a role model but I guess not any more. 'I worked until two last night,' Jason says. 'I'm so tired of it, I haven't had a break all year,' and the snakes in my hair hiss at him to fuck off.

Meanwhile that other dumb blond mugging from my smartphone. For weeks Johnson's been feeding titbits to the tabloids: *Christmas is Saved! Season's Meetings. A Very Covid Christmas. The Cost of Christmas. The Five Days of Christmas. The Twelve Rules of Christmas. So Here it is . . . Mini-Christmas. Tis the Season to be Jolly Careful.* The phonic similarities of 'bubbles' and 'baubles' have led to some puns that don't quite land.

The US election has been called for Biden; there have been vaccine breakthroughs. They could be celebrating now but instead the papers are nothing but Christmas – Christmas as distraction from the fact we still have no trade deal for Brexit; that Trump is trying to stage a coup; that people are dying. There's clearly going to be a brutal second wave and they're leaving it too late to do anything. Déjà vu.

Jason makes coffee. He says his colleague Alison's sister just died; she was only fifty-two. 'It's such a shitshow,' I say. He tells me I use the word 'shitshow' a lot these days. It's a passive-aggressive way of him telling me not to say 'shitshow' any more, it annoys him.

My mum doesn't want to see us over Christmas, she thinks it's too risky. She's just going to have Carol come over because 'she doesn't get out much'. Apparently, instead, it's been decided we're going to have Christmas with Jason's dad and girlfriend, his sister's family and their ninety-year-old grandmother. Jason seems unfazed. 'I need a holiday, okay? Maybe I actually want to see my family.'

'Advent is going to feel like a bomb ticking down. I mean, gatherings with your sister are normally tense but not ominous.'

'We'll be fine. My poor gran's hardly seen a soul this year.'

'For a party game, why don't we just bring a revolver with a single round in it then spin the cylinder?'

He laughs. 'Come on,' he says, softly, holding my shoulders, close with his breath. Trying to make a connection, I know, I know. 'You'll have a nice time, I promise.' Blasé, from the French, *blaser*, 'to cloy'; from French dialectal, 'to be chronically hung-over'.

Chresmomancy: Prophecy by the Ravings of Madmen

Trump is still demanding recounts, so that's a bad sign.

Brontomancy: Prophecy by Thunder

Aieeeeeeee!

A terrible sound wakes me and I stumble frantic to my feet, down the stairs. Xander has always been an early riser. When he was a toddler he'd wake us at four or five sometimes, crawling into our bed, wriggling sweet warm thing in bus pyjamas. Today he's been up two hours already playing games and when I get there he's broken because he failed to kill a Minotaur. I breathe. I need a wee. 'It doesn't matter, Xander, it's just a game,' I say. 'Here, you're hangry, have breakfast.' Soy milk splats over Shreddies.

'I'M NOT HANGRY, it's a DUMB WORD.'

Outside is still dark and the weather's wild, our bin knocked over. Broken pots. 'You shouldn't be playing before school anyway, it's a bad habit, I'm a bad mother for letting you. Please, don't cry, it's just a game.'

But he's gasping with snot, stomping and kicking and punching at himself. 'It DOES matter! If it doesn't matter NOTHING matters! It DOES MATTER!' A broken squealy roar.

I almost shout something back but then stop myself – there's no need, is there, to expose the futile pretence on which he has constructed his whole existence? The futile, convenient pretence. Like Jason says, I should pull my horns in. 'You need to get your uniform on,' I tell him at last, and he storms upstairs to his room.

'Alexa, play "Happy".' There's a blast of that smooth, foot-tapping music.

'Turn it down,' I shout up. I hate that fucking surveillance device in his room, I should never have let him have one for his birthday. Is there any moment he's not giving them data? It's so loud and I still have an email to do. Also neighbours. 'Xander, turn it DOWN NOW!' And he turns it off. He turns 'Happy' off.

Auramancy: Prophecy by Aura

> Everything is more beautiful because we're doomed. You
> will never be lovelier than you are now. We will never be
> here again.
>
> — Homer, *The Iliad*

I put a red cross next to this epigraph and write *reference?*
As it happens, the quote is from Wolfgang Petersen's
movie *Troy*, the one with Brad Pitt and Orlando Bloom,
but it's been uploaded as a Homer quote on Goodreads, a
little honeytrap for panicking essayists.

I hand in the marking and finish up for the term, go outside and wait for the bus, get on the bus, scrolling on my
phone. The war on the 'woke' continues – after all these
millennia the powerful have realized they can say that they
don't like conscious people. In fact, nationwide surveys
show most people strongly agree. Down with Awareness!
Cage the Cognizant!

Twitter says: *Week of 12/13 in Libra – Luck comes in a red hat.
Planning ahead is good, but so is letting someone else do the planning. Take the day and make a play of it.*

Sometimes, I still look at Jay on their Instagram feed: Jay's socks with little eyes; their chain over a black sweat; cat in a box at golden hour; Jay with two Instagram tears; angel in the cloud filter. Sometimes they use a filter that edges them in rainbow like an auric egg. They want someone to look, but is it me? I don't think it's me. I used to comment all the time, but I haven't for weeks. I still RT their Classics tweets, but that feels safer. Today I press the tiny ♡ and see red fill the chamber, and then feel like some disgusting old perv and want to take the red back, but would they see I'd unliked it, would that be worse?

An aura is a coloured emanation said to enclose a body, sometimes described as a human energy field. I've never seen one, although apparently once my dad said he saw one around my mum. It's one of those anecdotes about him – she was glimmering, the same but more beautiful, light spilling from her palms like a goddess . . . I don't recall a colour. Auras were popularized by Charles Webster Leadbeater, a member of the Theosophical Society. He framed himself as a scientist, but also claimed to have discovered that most men come from Mars, except for the more advanced ones, who come from the Moon. You can see his book *Thought-Forms*, written with Annie Besant, online. 'To paint in earth's dull colours the forms clothed in the living light of other worlds is a hard and thankless task,' the foreword opines. The plates are too beautiful. So many painters fell in love with them – Kandinsky, Mondrian, Beckmann. KEY TO THE MEANINGS OF COLOURS like a perfect watercolour palette: *High Spirituality* a pale indigo; *Strong Intellect* yolk gold; *Pride* coral; *Sympathy* like mint jelly; *Sensuality* a baked-clay red.

The auric eggs themselves are like lava lamps, ludicrously pretty. Zigzagged and striped as if candies for Easter. But then you read the labels beneath them more closely. *Plate VII: Astral Body of the Savage.*

Greek *aurā*, breath + *manteía*, prophecy. It's too easy to predict, that a colour chart where black represents *Malice* is going to end up misused; wielded by fascists who judge others for breathing. 'It is our earnest hope – as it is our belief – that this little book will serve as a striking moral lesson to every reader, making him realise the nature and power of his thoughts, acting as a stimulus to the noble, a curb on the base.'

When I get back it is four in the afternoon. Hermes and the Amazons have delivered parcels to our hallway, my Christmas shopping. Jason is drinking a beer in the nearly dark kitchen, himself and all our unwashed pots and pans silhouetted against the window, its pinky-red and dark-blue light. *Plate XVIII Deep Depression.*

'Where's Xander?' I ask.

'At the park, I think.'

Already I am panicking. 'Are you kidding me? You think? Where's his bag? Has he got his phone?'

'We had an argument, okay, I said . . .' I have to clench my jaw and fists; to make myself allow Jason to finish and not just run off after Xander that second. 'He wouldn't switch off the screen, he never listens to me. I told him this might be our last Christmas as a family. I told him you might leave me.'

'What?' I say. It is a genuine what, I didn't hear it properly, I feel like I heard it but didn't.

'You do know when you flirt on social media, it's all published? You know it's a public platform?'

'I haven't –' I begin, shrill, although I have. I think I mean to say: I haven't been looking at you properly. 'You're wrong,' I blurt. 'I'm not leaving you.'

'Okay, then,' he says, exhaling. 'Good. Okay. Thank you. Good.'

I'm trembling with readiness for the next blow; it can't be over so easily. But somehow it is. He pulls me towards him and softly kisses my head. And then he stoops to put on his jogging shoes and runs off stiffly towards the park, into the coming dark.

Micromancy:
Prophecy by Small Objects

'Millions will no longer be allowed to mix with other households at Christmas, as a new Tier 4 level of COVID restrictions comes into force. In a dramatic move, all those areas previously in Tier 3 in the South East – including London – moved to the new Tier 4 on Sunday, due to fears around a "mutant" strain. Pictures on social media this evening show panicking crowds at London's St Pancras station as people try to leave the capital before Tier 4 comes into effect. Seats on services to Newcastle are heavily booked.'

'I'm not telling Xander Christmas is cancelled,' he says, switching off the TV. 'I mean, is this for real? The state is saying I can't see my own father at Christmas?' And I – chastened, caught out, sorry, grateful for his mercy, frightened to cause any kind of scene in front of Xander – nod obediently and begin packing.

So we are in the car, heading to Jason's dad's place. It's late, I'm in the back, Xander is leaning on my shoulder in sleep, which is nice: his warm hair, his hand resting on me. The sound of wipers. Wet light hits black windows. Trickling light. With each soft breath Xander produces respiratory droplets that Jason and I inhale.

Dendromancy: Prophecy by Trees

'Hey!' The silver fox opens the door to greet us. We cross the threshold hurriedly, thinking of neighbours' eyes, but it is our hurry, not his. That self-satisfied smile. He hugs Jason. In the doggy hall, beneath the mistletoe, he kisses my cheek, which feels more invasive than usual. 'Saturnalia, eh! Time of reversals. Boris knows his Latin, doesn't he?' He's been saving this joke for me, and I'm supposed to be flattered.

'Yeah, we have a custom of electing a Lord of Misrule.'

'Ha, yes,' he smiles. He turns and high-fives Xander. 'Who's this young man, then?'

His girlfriend Helen's face hovers at the end of the corridor: sixtyish, blonde, beaming, her chin gone but still a beauty. 'Gin time!' she laughs convivially, going off to fix the adults their usual tray of icy, juddering drinks. Since retirement, they are creatures of ritual. There is always a bottle of decent red open, a crossword on the go, half a brown banana in the fruit bowl that Helen chops into muesli.

The house is legally Helen's, inherited, although Jason's dad has lived there a decade now. Old and draughty – the sort of house where wealth is strewn around carelessly, as though mundane. Fresh flowers in a chipped jug; a French painting above the wellies. Dogs largely stay in the kitchen, and when you open the kitchen door they leap on you. Christmas dinner is a side of beef, because turkey is disappointing.

Xander and I take the suitcases to our rooms. The sheets so cool and tucked in. We don't have a bath at home and I look at their bath greedily. It feels good, actually, to be somewhere different. 'Can I do Roblox with Jaden?' Xander asks.

'It's bedtime, love, get your jamas on and say goodnight to Grandad and Great-gran, okay? They're so pleased to see you. They haven't seen you all year.'

'They saw me in the summer at Grandad's party.'

'You know what I mean. They love you.'

In truth, they don't know how to interact with him now he doesn't want to get the toy box out. Jason's sister and her kids are not coming for Christmas after all and, padding down the staircase, I get the half-heard impression that she very much judges us for coming. But it's done now. Jason's granny is in the living room by the smoking fire, in the high-backed chair, waiting to receive us. She's very frail; communicates mainly in nods and smiles. Once, many years ago, she told me how she had to leave school at thirteen after her father had an affair. I know she has an inner life, this whole history – that I should talk to her properly, deeply – but I'm tired. I nod at her and smile. 'Nice tree,' I say.

'Helen did it,' Jason's dad interjects smoothly, poking a log into feeble sparks. 'Didn't she do a great job! Silver and cream, very classy. She did the wreath on the door too, didn't you, Helen? I said this year we should all have crosses instead!'

Jason is already moving on to red wine, twisting a cork-screw, his face looking strangely large and moist like it does when he's coming up. His father starts to elaborate plans. Long walks in boggy fields. A trip to Waitrose to stock up on Parmesan and salad, because the French are blockading the ports. The Addisons are coming over for supper. Why the fuck are the Addisons coming over? There's nothing a ten-year-old might enjoy. Everyone's politeness is stiff and unpractised.

It is Christmas Eve when I get the text from Jaden's mum, but I say nothing.

Drimimancy:
Prophecy by Bodily Fluids

Oxfordshire moves into Tier 4 on Boxing Day so we head home, Jason hung-over, drinking a can of Lilt as he drives. It's Xander who tells him, in the car. 'Jaden's got it.'

'Got what?'

'Covid – he says he's not got symptoms, though.'

'Right,' Jason says. 'Lucky, then.'

'I guess.'

When we get home I feel light-headed; slant. My sinuses feel strange: a pressure is building, like some giant hand is pressing down on my forehead, absolving me of something.

I don't dare say anything, just start to unpack. In the fridge is a bottle of curdled milk; a ragu I'd defrosted before we left in our hurry, now clammy grey. It's dinner time, I'll have to make them something out of something, but my stomach feels off. I begin to make them pasta, washing my hands very carefully first, very aware of my moist breath on the chopping board; the blade; the pepper. I chop my finger with the blade, drip blood. Plip. I shouldn't be doing this, I think, but I get through. 'I reckon I'll go to bed early,' I say, as I put the plates in front of them. I fill their waters and sway for a moment at the tap, clumsy-fingered, banging glass on metal. Nothing shatters but. Little floating lights in the corners of my eyes like I get when I'm stressed; like I can actually see the Covid cells in the air with their radiant spikes.

'Are you kidding, before Xander?' Jason asks. 'What, hangover is it?'

'I don't feel that good, to be honest.'

'Don't be ridiculous,' he snaps, because if he doesn't believe it then it isn't true.

'Do you feel okay, Xander?' I ask.

'Yes, Mum,' Xander replies, wearily. 'Yes, I feel okay.'

*

That night, I crawl off to the spare bed.

I wake at one and have to open the window. It's freezing outside but I feel this crazed thirst for fresh air, like I'll die without it.

The moon sits in the blur of her breath.

Sweat is pouring down me, I realize, all over my breasts like warm oil, sensuous, foul. The cold catches in my throat and I cough, trying to keep it quiet, not wanting to wake anyone.

The next day all my limbs are heavy. I drag myself to the bathroom and have a runny shit, and afterwards spray everywhere with the bathroom spray, rubbing and rubbing at the invisible particles, and open the window to let in more cold air. My pyjamas are soaked through, I have to change them. I stumble downstairs to make Xander his breakfast and he says, 'I've had my cereal already, Mum, you should rest,' so I go back to the bed with my phone for a week.

*

There's so much Christmas TV. So many lists shows. TV of the eighties and nineties. It's like they're saving those dying all the effort and unpleasantness of having to have their own lives flash before their eyes.

Jason has to drive me to a car park for a test, still saying it's probably just flu. As it brushes my tonsils, the swab makes me retch. Boris Johnson announces a new national lockdown.

Otherwise I stay in my sanctum, balanced over the fissure. Shaking. Am I afraid? The room is low and dark, a blood-thumping blur; filling with that decomposing smell, a sweet, crawling asphyxiant. My limbs jangle. The clump of my tongue.

Jason has to go to the hospital. His gran's very ill now. They've not got enough oxygen for everyone, there's a DNR. His dad and Helen are okay, although they can't taste wine. Jeffrey Addison's intubated. I'm not quite sure why Jason's allowed at the hospital but maybe he's just dropping off his gran's things or signing documents.

Xander puts the tray by my door: tea, slices of orange. I feel as though there is a pillow over my face. The nine swords glint and turn in screenlight. Why does radiant mean beautiful but incandescent mean furious?

When it's dark, Xander comes in and sits on the end of the sodden bed. 'Don't touch me,' I say, although I want to say don't worry. Or do I want to say don't help me?

Only then do I hear a very high, horrible squeak; see his face is creased into a sob. 'Great-granny's dead,' he shrieks, hitting himself. 'I killed her. I'm so dumb I'm so dumb . . .'

Adrenaline cuts through the stupor – I suddenly feel every droplet of sweat on my skin. I'm the oracle and I can see it, smell it: my son's future blackening and catching at the edges, bletting with black, spoiling, so I tear it from the flames with my hand –

'Don't be stupid,' I whisper, as lightly and calmly as I can. 'You don't even have the virus. We all know I'm the one who killed her.'

Phobomancy: Prophecy by Feelings of Fear

Trophonius was a hero or daimon or god, no one ever knew which. His name is from τρέφω *trepho*, 'to nourish'. Apollo, god of prophecy, was rumoured to be his father.

According to Pausanias, the second century AD traveller and geographer, Trophonius and his brother Agamedes built a treasure chamber for a king with a secret entrance only they knew about. Later, they snuck in and stole as much of the king's gold as they could carry. Unfortunately, greed led them to return to the scene of the crime. The second time, the king had laid a snare, and Agamedes was caught. In a moment of blind panic, Trophonius decided to chop off his brother's head, so the king would not recognize the body. Having done this, he fled to Lebadeia, where the earth opened and swallowed him.

Years later, plague struck the Lebadeians, devastating the land. Bodies piled up, heaped in mass graves without washing or dirges or libations. With no coins on tongues for the ferryman. People gnawing the air for air; pleading with the gods. *I'm not ready.* They consulted the oracle at Delphi, and the Pythia instructed them to find the grave of an unnamed hero and offer worship. 'Hero'! The word means 'protector' or 'defender' but has always been used interchangeably with 'violent man'.

At last, noticing bees pour into a fissure in the ground, a young shepherd followed them. He found Trophonius' cavern, and threw himself down in reverence. As predicted, the plague passed.

Pausanias relates many details about the cult of Trophonius. Consulting this oracle was perhaps even more complex than at Delphi. There was an endless list of rules. You had to stay in a particular house for a period of days; bathe; eat only sacrificial meat. Then there would be sacrifices to a series of gods – Cronus, Apollo, Zeus, Hera, Demeter – each made to a strict timetable. A ram was jostled into a pit for the shade of his brother, Agamedes. Water had to be drunk from the spring of Lethe, for forgetfulness, and Mnemosyne, for memory. Finally, dressed like a sacrificial victim, you would descend into the cave. A tug at the ankle; a swirling river; a blow to the skull; then the invisible creature spoke . . .

Everyone who went down into that cave experienced such terror they would come back up having forgotten what they were doing and everything that had happened. 'To descend into the cave of Trophonius' became a way of saying 'to suffer a terrible fright'. Emerging, they were ushered, catatonic, towards the chair of memory so that the priests of the shrine, so far as they were able, could prompt and record their froth of ravings.

Wait, though. What I wanted to say is that there is another version of the story, that I think about often. According to the 'Homeric Hymn to Apollo', Trophonius built the oracle's temple at Delphi with his brother, Agamedes. Once finished, the oracle told the brothers to do what they wished for six days and, on the seventh, their greatest wish would be granted.

On the seventh day, they were found dead.

Ichnomancy: Prophecy by Footprints

There's a list of schools going back, so we tell Xander he's going back, then it turns out he's not going back.

The next day Trump's supporters storm the Capitol. 'Proud Boys' with lead pipes; 'Oath Keepers' in army combat and helmets; 'God's Warriors'. They can't name anything without lying. They construct a gallows and noose; chant they want to hang Pence. Confederate flags. PELOSI IS SATAN. And Trump's family and friends watching it from some pissy, catered corporate tent.

We watch too, all of us, screens and phones both going as we spoon soup into our disbelieving mouths. Xander shaking his head, wow. Me thinking: *My prophecy, it's coming true! I'm a seer!* And also: *You and literally the whole commentariat, you pitiful dick.*

I am spared Jason's granny's funeral due to the limits on numbers. I imagine Jason must feel cheated, like I'm evading my punishment. I think perhaps I feel cheated of my punishment too. There's no wake. One morning Jason shaves and puts on aftershave, he and Xander put on dark coats and drive off. They don't say much when they get back. Xander goes straight up to his room and shuts his door.

After this, nothing else happens for weeks. Well, I say that but tens of thousands die and ambulances queue outside overwhelmed hospitals, it's just no one quite believes it this time; people hold up signs in hospital car parks saying COVID IS A HOAX and yell things like: 'This Isn't Happening!'

The lockdown is harder for us than the first; less novel. I'm out of dreaming pills. The school is under pressure to provide more teaching, so Xander has a Zoom assembly every morning, then two endless Teams meetings on mute, where the kids type expanded noun phrases into the comments box. Teams only works on my laptop and we can't work out how to switch off notifications or edit in doc. If anyone posts a smiley face emoji the headmistress's face pops up to explain sternly that this isn't social media. I try to work intermittently on my phone in the next room, but the extra device makes Teams buffer, and Xander doesn't engage unless I'm standing over him. It's a small victory when he reads a graphic novel on the toilet.

Every day I set up Xander at the computer, make him something to eat, try to work, help him with his assignment, buy something online, make him something to eat, wash up, try to work, phone my mum, make us something to eat, work in front of the TV. *A Perfect Planet, It's a Sin, The Dig, Call My Agent, The Serpent, Can't Get You Out of My Head.*

Someone wants this, I keep thinking. *Someone wants us to live like this.*

It's very cold outside. There's one morning of snow – the sky a blur of pixelated white – and Jason and Xander chuck a few snowballs. In a fat, pink snowsuit, the two-year-old from across the road stomps a labyrinth of tracks before forgetting they are hers and toddling after them. Pursues the monster of herself.

Jason orders more boxes of wine. He goes for a walk with Joey, who is apparently less manic, and claims he's been doing dry January, but they end up necking cans of beer on a frozen bench. It's hard not to be complicit with alcoholism when you really want a drink, I think, after he gets back, uncorking a Marlborough Sauvignon.

'We're not going to Delphi, are we, Mum,' Xander says that same evening, apropos of nothing.

Moromancy: Prophecy by Foolishness

In the Zoom waiting room, I ask myself what I want to get out of this. Why would I book a reading with Rae again?

But I do know, it's because her last reading was actually spot on. She predicted the danger that would hang in the air above me, that could kill me or kill. Covid-19, right? *And* she said the letter J was important, or Jay even. I tell myself that everyone knows – don't they, surely? – some kind of Jane or John in their family as a minimum, that if she'd said X it would have been more impressive. But part of me can't help but think it uncanny.

Still, after everything, I'm somehow in the exact same position as last year again. I feel this abject, poisonous need to know what's next. Am I waiting, I wonder, for her to say: 'You must leave your marriage'? Is that really the fucking level I'm working on, that I'll pay some shitty freelance actress in the hope they'll tell me 'you must leave your marriage' and make it seem like destiny? As if I'd leave him anyway. I'm incapable, on a cellular level, of doing anything to harm Xander. Also, perhaps I still love Jason, I just don't love us, and I'm the part of that I want rid of.

'Oh, hi, you again,' Rae says, when I come on the screen, obviously surprised to see me, which is not the best look for a psychic. Pushing her smooth blonde hair out of her face as she pulls out the pack and starts shuffling, knuckles brimming with ostentatious rings.

'Hi,' I say.

'Would you like to set an intention?' she asks with that edge of her voice frying.

'I just really need some kind of . . . future,' I say. 'I just want to know there's a future.'

What if Jason dies? I think suddenly; a nauseous lurch. What if he dies like my father died and it's just me left, responsible for everything? With addicts there's a time you can still choose your fate and then one day you might not even realize but the stars stick; the hexagram fixes. Haruspicy. Your fate is mapped in scars on your liver and can't be changed any more. GAME OVER.

'Yeah, it's natural, unprecedented times and all,' she replies, as though she has misheard me, beginning to lay cards down. 'You're blessed, but you're also going through a difficult period, am I right? You feel unsupported in this new lockdown, responsibilities are weighing on you, I know a lot of folks are finding it hard to stay hopeful.' Her patter. I feel a wave of déjà vu.

'What's going to happen with schools?' I ask suddenly. She should know if she's psychic. Rae smiles, her shiny beige lips tilting up at the corners.

'The children will be back soon, it's right not to rush. Now, back to *you*, don't be distracted, you're our focus today. You're allowed to be your own focus. You're worried about health, naturally, about your family's health. I see challenges ahead . . .'

She turns over The Hermit, stood in the snow. 'You feel very alone, don't you?' she observes. 'You keep it all bottled up. There's nobody you talk to. But The Hermit holds a lantern, that's your inner vision. Maybe you need this time with your thoughts, to learn something about yourself, to learn to be a better person.'

'Okay, I will,' I say, glad somehow to be told, lapping it up like a kitten with a bowl of milk. It's true. I am terribly lonely. She says the same to everyone, I know, but perhaps that's okay because perhaps we're all the same and it's what we all need to hear.

'Know thyself,' Rae declares; the Pythia at Delphi declares.

'Yes.'

'And this is the big one,' she says. 'What will be.' And then Rae turns over – of course she does – the Ten of Cups.

The rainbow, the loving couple, the happy children.

I flinch as though at the spring of a trap. 'Domestic bliss,' she says. 'Lucky you.'

Batrachomancy: Prophecy by Frogs

Xander has developed a little chirrup, a squeak like a hinge that needs oil, which I suppose he finds comforting. I find it heartbreaking. Jason finds it annoying and keeps snapping at him: 'They'll think you're a freak at school.'

'I'm not at school, though, am I?'

Jason finds it annoying that I don't stack the plates in the right order; that when I shower, the bathroom floor is always a bit wet. He implies it's annoying I was so stupid as to get ill and infect his family. I find it annoying that I only did so because I was doing what he wanted, against my better judgement, but he never acknowledges that. I'm annoyed he never just calls me a murderer and we could get it out in the open at least. I'm annoyed by how long he sits on the toilet; the talk radio he listens to; the sound of him exercising; how I can never find the scissors. I'm annoyed his water glass smells like vodka. I'm annoyed Xander eats a snack then hands me the wrapper, like I'm a bin. Xander finds my Ancient Greek facts annoying now: *Yes, I know eighty per cent of Athenians were slaves, Mum.* He's annoyed by the fact I've set a screen-time limit so his tablet locks after an hour. I'm annoyed

I have to be this person in this body at this fucking historical moment.

We all seem to snap more frequently, get tearful. Silly little fights.

One morning, Xander's assignment is to watch a BBC Bitesize on endangered species then make a poster about them – freshwater dolphin, gibbon, tiger, sloth, pangolin. He begins with a ghost frog, crackle-eyed. They've evolved to wave at females instead of croak, as the waterfalls are so loud.

'Jaden says pangolins started the lockdown,' Xander notes, starting to draw the intricate scales. A smudge of blue pen on his forehead, like mould. 'It's pangolin disease.'

'I don't think so,' I reply, in an ill-informed hurry, not wanting him to ponder the intricate paths of damage; to follow the thread of that thought.

'Poor cute little pango,' Xander says, giving his pangolin big eyes.

If this is a game, what do the programmers want? When you think about evolution as a process; when you think about how humans have thrived in this world, a species whose every individual is so completely unique; when you think about entropy ... The aim is clearly to develop complexity. But as I help Xander google facts I realize there's some glitch in the programme now, isn't there? Suddenly, this world is crashing; simplifying. Diminishing. The gods must be so sad.

*

A miracle occurs: they don't fuck up the vaccine roll-out. Even my mum has her jab (although she complains on the phone, because it's Pfizer, and what about the second dose? Her paper says Europe are going to block them through spite). At last the schools are going back. There's an atmosphere of elation, everyone at the school drop-off is smizing above their masks. Mums joshing on Whats App: *you think your kids are excited, wait until you see the nits' kids!* Xander is in his uniform, the trousers suddenly short on his ankles, walking out of the hell of this year and through the gates into normality.

Except it isn't over, quite, it doesn't stop. When I pick him up at half three, there are so many parents chatting, not wearing masks, and prams, and reception kids running into my legs I feel hassled by the proximity to bodies. I overhear two of the mums saying anti-vax things – 'Just google the swine flu jab, it gave all these kids narcolepsy.' We're still in full lockdown too; there's still a stay-at-home order. The *Guardian* runs articles on coping with the end of lockdown but it's an entire month before we can even step into a friend's garden; a minimum six weeks to a haircut. I feel gaslit by this idea we've made it through.

Meghan and Harry are interviewed by Oprah, and no one talks about anything else for a few days. The Graeae stare transfixed through their single eyeball.

*

It keeps coming, though, more history, spewing from the pipe. Sarah Everard, who was walking home at 9 p.m. near Clapham, is found dead. A vigil is staged: girls and flowers. In my twenties I'd have been there – I remember standing at protests with my banner stuck to a broom handle, written in sharpies:

> OF ALL CREATURES THAT
> CAN FEEL AND THINK,
> WE WOMEN ARE THE WORST
> TREATED THINGS ALIVE
> – Medea

I've been whistled at, groped, though it was long ago when I was someone else and the memories are not ones I've returned to for years. I consider going to the vigil but don't, I don't know why. Perhaps because I don't feel like an innocent victim any more – feel too guilty and tarnished and complicated to express such righteous indignation. Or maybe it's the thought of all those bodies near me, or that dream about the prison cell, or the fact I don't post on Instagram. The police pin a masked Antigone to the floor.

A sudden hailstorm that weekend, like a stoning.

The second reading of a bill I only just hear about now, on Twitter, when it's already too late. How is it all happening so fast? This government want any protestors causing 'annoyance' to be locked up for ten years. It's targeted at Black Lives Matter and Extinction Rebellion; at young people. That sense of the teeming world diminishing again knocks me over with a wave of sickness; sea's churn over dead coral. I sign an online petition that will make no difference and realize it will be Xander in that cell, not me.

But what about me, right? What did Rae say? I'm allowed to be my own focus. Self-care. Me Time. I actually have some minutes of my own, though, so I make an effort: light a scented candle, do a ten-minute yoga video, all the treats I'm legally allowed as a middle-aged woman in 2021.

Afterwards I sit to write at the kitchen table, with a couple of wondrously clear hours, deciding to finally actually begin the prophecy book, although it's hard to start. To write anything requires this ludicrous confidence in the future – that it exists, and contains a person who might read my words with interest.

Aichmomancy:
Prophecy by Sharp Objects

A year since the first lockdown began. The Prime Minister has a press conference. His main regret is that he didn't know then what he knows now.

The next day I pop into the office to collect some stuff and work at another desk for an afternoon. Xander is meant to be walking back with a friend. But when I get home Jason is on his laptop with a beer in his hand, listening to the cricket through headphones as he types. He doesn't hear me come in. I wash my hands thoroughly, although I stopped singing 'Happy Birthday' around June. 'Where's Xander?'

'I thought you were picking him up,' he says.

'Why?' I say. 'You know he's been walking back with Jaden some nights.'

'Oh right.'

'Oh right? Jesus, Jason.'

'Okay, what do you want me to say? Fucking hell it's an emergency he's probably dead? He'll just be in the park again.' I wonder why Jason doesn't leave me. I start to phone Xander but he doesn't pick up.

'Hey this is Xander's disembodied voice,' says the voice-mail. 'Leave me a message!'

'It's Mum, could you call please, we thought you'd be home by now,' I say. Jason pulls on his trainers.

'Can you check location on his phone?' he asks. 'I think you can, can't you?'

'How?' I ask, helpless. Is that a thing?

'Oh, never mind, I'll find him.' He jogs off as I phone Jaden. That single magpie in the garden fuck it. The ring-tone. *Pick up, pick up.*

'Jaden, hey, it's Xander's mum, is Xander with you?'

'Nah, I go to my dad's house Mondays.'

'Oh, okay, we thought he might be with you, do you know who he's with?'

'Just on his own, I think. I didn't talk to him today really.'

'It's just he's not home yet. You'll let me know if he calls you?' I say as serenely as I can.

'Yeah, course, miss.' *Miss.* Like I'm his teacher.

He's not with Tyler either. He's not in the park on the way home from school. Jason phones to say he's jogging over to another park to check there. It will be nothing, he promises, don't cry, it will be okay. I phone the school, who mention the police. The police think it's too early, he'll probably come home a bit late, maybe he bumped into some other friends? Is he depressed? Was there anything different about him this morning? Is anything missing from the house, any clothes or supplies? I think about gangs. The value of his trainers. Knives. His phone. Boys bleeding out on stairways.

I feel my life rushing away from me, like my soul has been torn out of my fingers by a river and it's disappearing from view.

And then Jaden calls me back. 'Miss,' he says. 'You should look on his Instagram, on his private Insta.'

'What?' I ask, pitifully, ignorant that he had more than one. 'Can you read it to me, or – or send me a screenshot maybe? And DM him, tell him to get in touch?'

'Yeah, I mean. Well it's just a video. You know that one "Dumb Ways to Die"?' And I do know it: the little smiling pastel blobs who are decapitated or exploding. Earworm of the summer. *So many dumb ways to die.* I think I let out a moan as I hang up because I know it's the dumbest dumbest stupidest suicide note I've ever heard, my darling boy.

Think, THINK. Xander's not picking up because it's me, I think, I'll try to call him from something else, another device. So I grab the old iPad from the lounge with shaking fingers and try to FaceTime him on that and then it works – it connects – and I can hardly see him in that somewhere, which is dark and grainy. The realm of Hades. And Xander, my son, laughs a deadpan laugh when he sees who I am and then reaches to switch me off again and I can see his wrists, streaked in the dark with blood, and I hate that screen so much, that thief, I want to shatter the iPad howling and crawl through the smashed screen into that place where he is, but he's gone. Swallowed by the screen's neck.

It takes me too many seconds to realize what I needed to realize minutes ago.

Tragedy is all about Unity of Place.

He's not out there, there's nowhere he's allowed to go – nowhere that wants him. He's here, I realize, in the house, in this cursed fucking house, where he always is. The crawl space in the eaves! And I'm bounding up the stairs like some maenad, crazed, screeching his name –

*

The observer effect proposes that the attempt to observe something causes it to change.

Until I open the door of the cupboard and look at him, then, Xander is neither alive nor dead.

One of my selves pulls it open and the *ekkyklêma* reveals the moist kitchen knife – *Look at it steadily; come closer to the truth –*
]
]

Poor bitch! She is too late now he is lost . . . no breath, no aura, it is intolerable . . .

NO NO COME BACK she's breathing into him [] [] [] begging; trying to scream herself out of her skin, out of her destiny –

GAME OVER GAME OVER

But this is not her story. Somehow, I am the lucky self who has a different fate: who finds her son whimpering, breath still inflating his lungs. I am the self who wraps his cuts with his baby blanket, who dials 999, who hears the siren song outside the house, footsteps up the stairs.

I get to kiss his still-chirruping head; whisper *I love you stay.*

Dactylomancy: Prophecy by Means of Finger Movements

It is so quiet in our living room, weirdly silent, as though the whole of the world outside is on fire.

Xander is resting on the couch. Brown curls on the cushion, tired eyes, a damp cheek. Since Jason drove us back from the hospital we both keep checking him, like we can't believe he is still here. Is this our son?

Jason is in the kitchen making him a sandwich. 'Shall I turn on the TV?' I ask. 'Do you want your games?' Because I only want him to be happy.

'Not really,' Xander says.

'What would you like, then? Anything you like, anything.'

'Just tell me a story, Mum, like you used to.'

'Okay,' I say, moved, almost sick with nostalgia, perching next to him on the couch. When I take his hand, I feel his fingers curl around mine, the brush of his swaddled wrist. His nails are still bloodied; I notice the lifeline on his palm is long. I want to pray to someone: *Please, make this meaningful, make this a sign.*

'According to tradition,' I begin, swallowing, 'the Sibylline Books were bought from the Cumaean Sibyl by the last king of Rome, Tarquin the Proud. At first, when she offered Tarquin nine books of these prophecies, he said the price was too high. So she burned three and offered the remaining six to him at the same price. But the king was stubborn, and he refused, again, still hoping for a better deal. The Sibyl smiled at him, set fire to three more, and repeated her offer as they flared and guttered. Only then did Tarquin understand. He purchased the last three at the full original price.'

Acknowledgements

I have wanted to be a novelist for a very long time, and am very grateful to all who supported me through the years of rejections. Thanks are due to many people who have helped with this book. To my mum, who has encouraged me to make up stories all my life. To Hannah, who has been my friend and reader for over twenty years. To my agents: Jenny Hewson, for her continued belief in my work, and Lucy Carson in the US. To the Society of Authors for a work-in-progress grant. To Helen Garnons-Williams and Lauren Wein, for giving me this chance, and for making the editing of this book such a pleasure. Thanks also to Kyiah Ashton, Amy Guay, Karen Whitlock for copy-editing, and Fiona Benson for letting me quote her wonderful poetry collection *Vertigo & Ghost*.

I am not a classicist or an academic, and most of my research for this book was done piecemeal and online during the pandemic. Any errors are my own.

The book is not a description of my own family or our lockdown. Gratitude to all my friends, and especially Lorna and Anna for their company during the bleakest weeks. And thank you, always, Cate, Gruff and Richard for the love and the kitchen discos.